THE CASE OF THE
RAINFOREST REUNION

Jim Shon & Masa Hagino

HAWAII
INSIGHT
BOOKS

HONOLULU, HI 96822
United States

Contents

More books available
at
https://hawaiiinsightbooks.com

The Case of the Good Deed
$3.99 – $9.99

The Case of the Rainforest Reunion
$3.99 – $9.99

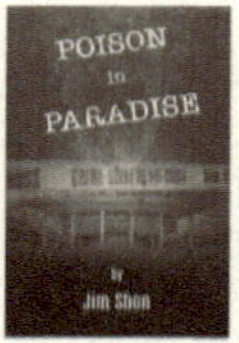

Poison in Paradise
$3.99 – $9.99

Hawaii Insight Books
Broadening Your Perspective

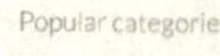

Popular categories

New Releases

Soon

Mystery

Politics

Useful links

About

Books

Blog

Civic Education

Contact

PROLOGUE

The human history of Makiki-Tantalus is long, extensive and diverse A state archaeological survey of Makiki Valley in 1980 revealed numerous prehistoric agricultural sites Th e early Hawaiians grew taro in the swampy land near the valley mouth, where runoff from Tantalus collected, and on the small alluvial fl ats along the streams Legend tells of sweet potato gardens grown on Round Top, whose Hawaiian name, Pu'u 'Ualaka'a means "hill of the rolling sweet potato."

Water was plentiful Although few native food plants existed in Hawai'i, the pioneering settlers brought with them food crops which grew readily in this new fertile land Hawaiian introductions included taro, sugarcane, sweet potato, breadfruit, mountain apple, banana, ti and kukui Plants that provided fuel, building material, medicine, fi ber and dye grew in the upper valley and mountain Forest birds and land snails were plentiful.

Dramatic change arrived with Westerners Introduced livestock such as horses, cattle, goats and pigs began to destroy the forest understory and compact the soil From 1815-1826 the sandalwood trade with China virtually eliminated this native tree from the area A single ship's hold could carry more than 6,000 trees at one time!

By the late 1800s most of Makiki was bare, denuded of trees. The native forest was gone.

The barren hillsides became heavily eroded, and both the quantity and quality of fresh water in the streams below declined. In 1893 the Kingdom of Hawai'i formed a Commission of Agriculture and Forestry. In 1903 this became the Territorial Board of Agriculture and Forestry. The Board acquired upper Makiki Valley in 1904, and began a much-needed reforestation effort in 1910.

Tantalus has long been a favorite locale of summer homes for those wishing to escape the summer's heat.

Today, Tantalus provides a much-loved retreat from the bustling city. New trails and look-outs have opened up the area for hikers, joggers, mountain bikers, picnickers, people out to enjoy the view and Hawai'i Nature Center students learning to love and care for the forest. Yet a hiker would find few native plants. He'd be surrounded mostly by imported, invasive, non-native plants.

One of the most aggressive, and widespread, was bamboo.

* * *

He studied the pictures from the Internet. Since he was younger he'd become fascinated with bamboo. His trip to Kyoto in college led him from temple to temple. He took hundreds of pictures of fences, screens, bamboo groves. But what caught his eye the most was the New Year's *kadomatsu*. A *kadomatsu* (門松?, literally "gate of pine") is a traditional Japanese decoration of the New Year placed in pairs in front of homes to welcome ancestral spirits or *kami* of the harvest. Three large bamboo shoots are set at different heights and represent heaven, humanity, and earth – bound at the bottom with straw rope, with pine or other branches as further decoration. *Kadomatsu* are placed in pairs on either side of the gate, representing male and female. He'd seen a local arts company selling them in Honolulu, but never really paid attention before.

A chance meeting with a carpenter at a Kyoto craft store taught him about the different specialized saws used. A fairly wide toothed one to cut the bamboo itself, but a much more finely toothed saw was needed to slice the tops at the sharp angles, making a clean and neat cut. He brought some back from his trip, determined to learn how to do it himself.

Not particularly religious, he did not care so much for the traditional purposes, the spirits or kami, the New Year ceremonies to honor and receive the deity, who will then bring a bountiful harvest for farmers and bestow the ancestors' blessing on everyone. After January 15, the *kadomatsu* is burned to appease the *kami* or *toshigami* and release them.

For him, it was more of a vague sense of respect and remembrance. He started by making his crude versions and placing them on the grave of his grandmother. Seemed nicer than just flowers, he thought. But recently, he had a special purpose. For several years, he would hike up into the hills above Honolulu, cut the bamboo, and fashion a *kadomatsu*. He would reverently place it along the trail, near the bench that was positioned to enjoy the upper Manoa hills. Often the previous year's *kadomatsu* was still there, off in the bushes.

It was personal. It was private. He didn't care if anyone else knew, or saw it, or appreciated it. It was his gift to a memory. Yet it was noticed. He found comfort in working with his hands. Those times when he just could not seem to get out of bed, and when he needed to take his meds but spent his money on bar hopping, he found solace in making his *kadomatsu*. It was his therapy. And it helped keep his memory of her alive. So sad. She may never have loved him. And yet, somehow he was speaking to her. Expressing something deep inside.

* * *

Zoe Lee, award winning reporter for the on-line *Manoa Investigator*, placed the small bouquet on the modest grave marker of Kirk Daniels in Oahu Cemetery. Her one and only love. It had been two years since his untimely death. The Case of the Good Deed, they called it. Her biggest success. Her biggest sorrow.

Hey Kirk. Sorry, haven't been in touch for two weeks. You know how this newspaper is, always wanting today's story yesterday. You wonder what I'm working on? Yes. You always were interested in my life, my thoughts, my passions. This is why we found each other, don't you think? Well, I'm not doing anything about developments in Kakaako, I can tell you that. After we closed down the Shilling Development guys, I thought it best to leave it alone, you know. Our last great success. Often wonder what we would have accomplished had…things been different. Often wonder what unbelievable issues you would have drawn me into.

Well, these days I'm looking into the drug culture of Hawaii. Starts often in middle school. Yes, meth, heroin, but now these prescription opioids. Kids get them from the parents. Parents get hooked on their own, or in the hospital. It is everywhere. Heard about my friend's cousin, do you remember Liz? Well her cousin died of an overdose.

Yeah, I know I'm changing the subject. How am I? I really don't know most days. Took up Hula to keep my mind off things. It's really physical. I've met new friends. No, I mean girlfriends, silly. But, Kirk, I can't go a day or night without thinking of you. Nights are worse. Sorry about these tears. No, I'll be OK. Brought you your favorite flowers, the blue ones. The ones.. the ones… that matched your eyes. Bye baby…

Main Characters

Charlie C. Chang – a Honolulu Police Detective

Joe and Molly (Mai Tai) Davis – owners and managers of a small walk up apartment

Yoshiro "Moto" Fujimoto – a restaurant owner

Michael Furutani, Chair of the Police Commission, Businessman

Arthur Kido, Police Chief

Julie – a bar owner in Chinatown

Zoe Lee – a young reporter

Clare Song – the Head of a forensic investigation lab

Kono – Shilling's assistant

Zoe Lee – a young reporter

Tako Bob – alias for a cybersecurity consultant

Senator Byron Wakayama – Representing the Makiki Tantalus district

The Grover Cleveland High School Class of 94

Ben Flores – Unemployed

Sabrina Matsumoto – Former Waikiki waitress

Sarah Taira – lives in Punchbowl condo; divorced, practices criminal law

Wendy Gushiken – lives in Manoa, is a chef at the Pacific Club, husband is a banker.

Maya Kai - lives in Waipahu, owns a small accounting firm, single.

Judy Conlin – single, lives in Helena Montana, runs outdoor adventure tours;

Gary Hoe – lives in Waianae; teaches math at Leeward Community College

Reed Radcliff – lives in San Francisco; investment advisor for futures stocks

Shirley Garcia – lives in Kalihi; works as a physical therapist at the Rehab Hospital;

Eileen Kerrigan – lives in Syracuse, NY, manages IT systems at Lemoyne College

Will Kalaiopula - lives in Makiki, works for State Department of Land and Natural Resources,

Jake Kim – lives in Hawaii Kai, Pharmacist at HealthRite Drug Store;

Jarrett Tanji – Lives in Pearl City, Used car salesman; divorced

Jason Menor – Lives in Los Angeles, plays soccer for the LA Galaxy

IT'S WHO YOU KNOW

June 1. 2014

Ringgg!

"Oh Shadda up!"

Ringgg!

"Forget it, I gotta get this out!"

"Damn phone!" Chang yelled." Keeps ringing all day. How am I going to finish my report. What did Moto-san call it: The case of The Broken Parakeet. Kaa-razy Japanee!"

Ringgg!

To Chang, it seemed even louder than the first three rings. "Hmmm, this can only mean…."

"Hello Chang here. *This better be good*. Oh, hello Chief. Inspector Chang here and ready to serve." Police Chief Arthur Kido took pride in bragging that he was on top of every case. Yet Chang knew it was not really true. Kido tended poke his nose where he had some personal interest.

"Yes, I am certainly willing to talk to the Chair of the Police Commission. Should I come over. Oh, he wants to first ask me a few questions." Kido transfers the phone to Furutani.

"Oh, hello Mr. Furutani. We officers are all appreciative of your backing up our work and personally lobbying the City Council on our budget."

"Thank you for your willingness to talk to me," said Furutani, formally. "I know how busy you are. The Chief just told me how you wrapped up this murder case just last night and you promised him a final report before lunch. Well, Mr. Chang, you just might have another case to solve. No, it hasn't made the papers yet. It has not made the media as a homicide. At first, it was treated just as an unfortunate tragedy, involving some hikers up on Tantalus. Know the area?"

"Oh yes, Chair Furutani. I live just one valley over. And when I was younger I hiked all over Manoa, Round Top, Nuuanu."

"Well, Inspector, tell me, what school did you graduate from?"

"Well, Chair Furutani, you are speaking to a proud graduate of the public school system---McKinley High School.

Now, Chang thought. If it was any place but Hawaii when someone asked what school you're from, it assumed they meant from what college did you graduate? What alma mater, collegiate wise. But this was Hawaii. They wanted to know the name of your high school. Personal relationships, including family, all seemed to emanate from your high school origins. Ah, sighed Chang, the traits and genetics of living on an island. Only we Asians, especially the Chinese, still honor our ancestors and place greater weight on our origins. In America some of that is being lost.

Chang thought about his own grandchildren and how none of them speak more than a few phrases of the old language, and how they had to be dragged to the cemeteries for ceremonies to honor the deceased. *And none of them became practicing Buddhists.*

"And so, Inspector Chang!" Jarred back to real world, Charlie picked up the train of words, "When the autopsy was done it was revealed that the cause of death was not heart attack or stroke or some form of exhaustion from the hike, but from *poison*. The victim's name is Ben Flores. He was poisoned. And it was not food poisoning. Someone poisoned him. It had to be deliberate. It had to be murder. But who?"

"Forgive, Mr. Chairman. He died of poison, yes. I leave that to the doctors and the medical examiner. But we detectives must first gather all the evidence, then study and make the determination."

Chang heard the Chair change his tone of voice and it became more subdued. "Oh, yes, Mr. Chang, I did not want to step into your arena. You are correct as always. We leave that up to you."

Good, thought Chang. You must let people know who's in charge here. Even if he is the almighty Chair of the Honolulu Police Commission. And why does the Chair, or any Commissioner, have any particular interest in any particular case? Unless there's family involved or maybe some business partner.

He listened as the Chair went on. "I have asked about your school because, you see, it involves a high school reunion and I wanted to make sure you wouldn't have to deal with your classmates. So, why don't you come over to the Chief's office. I'll tell you more then. At least, I'll tell you what I know."

C H A P T E R   2

A CLASS ACT

June 1. Same Day

As Chang walked into the Chief's office, he immediately noticed the snappily dressed business executive. Not a wrinkle anywhere on his suit, shirt, tie, or even his pants. *I wonder what this cost?* Chang mused to himself, just a little jealous. *Everyone knew about Michael Furutani. Big time stock trader, ownership of Top Flight Cars, all with foreign names,* Chang reflected. *The biggest yacht in the islands and offices all over the world, yet he spends much of his time in Hawaii, where he was born and raised. His parents had come from Japan to open branch offices and stores for the father's parent company – a big zaibutsu. Now he is Chairman of the Police Commission.*

"Ah, inspector Chang! Thank you so much for taking the time. We've met twice before I believe." Furutani was so quickly out of his chair and to speak that he even beat the Chief to it. "The Commission honored a number of officers for their splendid job in protecting the people of Oahu. I recall you were honored for solving three cases. Now let me see what name did the media give to them. The Case of the Tuna Boat Mystery, The Case of The North Shore Surfer, and, most recently, The Case of the Good Deed. Great and descriptive names." Furutani noticeably cringed when he mentioned the last one, for it involved a corrupt police officer, and required a special investigation by the Commission.

Chang was amazed at the Chair's memory, and said so. "You do me the honor of remembering these rather insignificant cases. I had more time than the detectives in which to crack them open."

The Chief butted in, "Oh come on Chang, you know the other detectives had one for over a year and another one faked out three other detectives who took turns in solving it and over a 5-year period as I recall. What did it take you? And The Good Deed, taking down the corrupt developer Shilling. I should ask for your autograph."

"Oh no, Chief," Chang said with false modesty, "you know those were busy times and everyone had some other cases to crack. I was just lucky."

"Have you ever been unlucky?" Furutani asked. "You pretty much single handedly put a major developer in jail, and helped a Hawaiian family recover their land in Kakaako. It will go down in history as one of the great feats of law enforcement!"

"The Gods smile on me. And I hope they continue to do so. At least until I retire." *Boy, this man can really shovel it, thought Chang. Why is he buttering me up?*

The Chief interjected: "Well, don't you retire before I do. You make me look good. And I don't mind saying that in front of Chairman Furutani."

"Well, Inspector, I won't take too much of your time. I thought it was an opportunity to meet with you in person. The Chief will give you the file. But I wanted you to hear directly from me why I've taken a personal interest in this case of murder."

Chang put on his blank face, refusing to react to the preconceived conclusion.

"I had asked about your school Inspector Chang, because the people involved, that is, all those around at the time of death, are all friends and in fact classmates of the victim, who attended Cleveland High. I had attended the same school a few years earlier, but we all knew each other. Yeah, you know how it is growing up on a small island - all the same school kids tend to hang out together even if they go to separate colleges later on. In fact, all of the boys in that group and I played baseball together in the young adult leagues. Well, it was me against the other six guys back then."

"But you know how it is in the islands. I wanted to make sure you didn't go to the same school because you would surely know them or their brothers and sisters if you had attended the same school, even though you were not in the same class. I did not want to risk compromising the investigation. You know the local mentality here."

Chang reflected: *I sure do. Local yokel. No doubt in my mind. Cultural comfort food, but it does at times grow tedious. Hawaii is a different place now. It is time to outgrow some of those small kid time habits.*

As he handed Chang the file, the Chief explained: "The file has the names and what biographies we have of the victims and the others who were witnesses. They all had come into town for their class reunion. The reunion was over, but since about five or six of the now mainland guys had not been home in a number of years, they had decided to stay an extra week to hang out. For the people involved, it was mainly their old group---yes, they all hung together in high school."

The Chief continued, going over the same points again and again. *I've got to resist rolling my eyes,* thought Charlie. "So they spent time with family and with making up for decades of lost time with old friends and lovers. Some of them did go to college together. Five did return and, of course, those five did socialize here. You know, Oahu Country club for golf, the Pacific Club for business and social events."

Chang interrupted and turned to the Chairman. "How is it that you, Mr. Furutani, are personally involved, at least to this point of asking me that question of school ties and meeting with the Chief? Not precisely your kuleana, responsibility or interest at the lofty Commission level."

"You're right," Furutani said.

The Chief butted in. "I can speak to that. As you know, there was a time when Commissioners would often get involved in department affairs and calling for a friend, or a friend of a friend. Well, the police chiefs beginning with two of my predecessors had called."

"Thanks Chief," said Furutani. "I can honestly say, Inspector Chang, that I have never called on any Chief or cop for any kind of special request. In fact, my only reason from coming here is that I wanted the Chief to assign his very best man to the case. It was a case that might have gone unnoticed and assigned to whomever was available or to whomever was next in line. No, I wanted the very best from the outset. Yes, I take special concern for this because I know the people who went on the hike and one of them, Ms. Gushiken, called me and told me how distraught she was. She's even more special to me, though we had not seen or even kept in touch with each other for the last twenty years. The usual excuses: family, business, professions; she's an interior designer."

Old high school sweetheart, I bet, Chang thought. Might follow up on this later.

Furutani went on. "All of the mainland people are so affected by the tragedy that they're staying for the memorial service. Part of the service is the scattering of the ashes, out at the surf at Magic Island. Ala Moana Bowls was one of his favorites, if not his very favorite, surfing site. His friends will be in one canoe and his family in the other for that traditional farewell ceremony."

"So, Mr. Chang, it's my hope, though I know how long these investigations can take, that you might be successful in solving this mystery before the mainland people have to leave. It will help to bring closure for them and for all of us who knew Ben. I just want to rest easy and to comfort Wendy, ah, Ms. Gushiken, that we are sparing no effort in catching whomever is responsible."

Chang whistled and thought *Yeah! We goin' catch this buggah!*

"Well, this is a tall order, Mr. Furutani, but Inspector Chang will certainly do his best," assured the Chief.

"Do you have any questions for Chairman Furutani? He has some business meetings to attend."

"Oh no, Chair Furutani. I will have questions, but let me go through the file first. I need the backgrounds of the hikers, and the vic's dearest friends from high school." Chang thought to himself with sarcasm, *well, someone likely killed him. First the background.*

"Here's my card, Inspector. Feel free to call me. I even wrote my personal phone number on it, and you can call me at any time, day or night. With that I'll leave the two of you."

Furutani exited. Chang turned to face the Chief, as he was handed the file. It was thin. Chang didn't even bother to open it then.

"Well, Chief, any thoughts? Any ideas how this could have happened?"

"Oh, no, Charlie C. Chang. You're not going to get me to speculate. Every time I've done so when it's still early in the game, you've gone on to surprise me. Not this time. Especially when the Chair has shown his personal interest."

"Yes Chief, and I am still a little surprised. Not that he would have shown interest, but that he would make a personal trip here. *But then, he must have nothing to do with the murder. After all, why would he, to use his own words, not want the very best?* Chang thought to himself suspiciously.

"Okay, that's it Chang. Unless you got questions, get out and do your job."

"I'm going up to Tantalus this afternoon, or at least when I finish this report for the first case. You'll be wanting it as soon as possible, I assume Chief."

"There you go, Chang. No, this case has precedence and you can do that report after you solved this one. Why can't you just ask me if you can postpone? You try to get me to say what you want in the first place."

As Chang exits, he hears his now vexed Chief, "And don't you give this case another fancy and catchy name. We're a police department, and you're a cop, not some movie script writer, or is it movie star?"

* * *

The Chief waited to be sure Chang was out of ear shot. He speed-dialed on his personal smart phone.

"Senator Byron Wakayama speaking. How can I help you?"

"Yo, Byron, Arthur here."

"Oh, Chief. Can I call you back on my private phone?" Beep beep. "This is better, more private. So did you meet with Chang and Michael?"

"Yeah, we met. Chang will be lead on the case, but we will be watching closely."

"You know, Arthur, I wouldn't be leaning on you, but it is my district, and I need a heads up on whatever happens. I've got a reelection coming up, and my opponent is hammering me for being soft on drugs and crime, and…."

"Yes Byron, I know, I know. I'll try to keep this low profile. Yes, I know we don't need another scandal or media circus. Yes, I will give you a heads up if anything breaks. Yes, Byron. Yes. Talk to you soon."

C H A P T E R   3
TAKE A HIKE CHARLIE CHANG!

June 1. 3 pm

Charlie was in his beloved De Lorean going up Tantalus. *I just love this drive. How long has it been since I've been up here? Just too busy at work. Let me see, it must be at least five years or more since the last drive. It always seems so sunny when I come up. The light is somehow brighter and everything seems cheery and the city, when you look down at It, looks so clean.* The 8-mile two-lane paved winding road had been built between 1914 and 1917, in part to enhance access to a growing number of wealthy summer homes built to escape the hot weather. *The rich always can get government to do their work,* he thought.

He turned into the Puu'Uala Park entrance, drove up the hill to the parking lot. He walked to a small look out – built especially for visitors and locals to enjoy the view. The lookout gave anyone a great view of Manoa Valley and even down to Waikiki, and of course Diamond Head. There were two others - a couple with bright orange sunburns on their cheeks, arms and legs.

"Aloha, you must be tourists. Where are you from?"

"We're from the Midwest. Indiana", the man said. The woman added: "South Bend to be exact."

"Ah Notre Dame! I have a nephew that went there."

"How great! My husband here is a professor at Notre Dame. We're on his sabbatical. He promised me when we got married that even though we couldn't afford a honeymoon here in paradise that we would someday make it. But you know how it is, there's the kids and working for tenure…"

"But here we are" - the husband interrupted - giving her a kiss."

"Happy honeymoon. Oh, and since you are a professor, you know you can see the University of Hawaii Manoa campus there."

The tourist looks down the valley. "It's bigger than I had imagined it to be."

Chang walked back to his car and drove off. After a half mile stretch, he hit the rest of the road with its roof of monkeypod trees. It was so thick that he always felt he was in a tunnel.

Chang was surprised when he first read about how the local boy from Hawaii, who got himself elected president of the United States, wrote that when he was growing up here, Puu Ualakaa was his favorite park, and he had often come here. *Just like me!*

Chang parked his car at one of the turnouts facing east, including Manoa, Diamond Head, and parts of Waikiki. He took in the best view of the city, in his opinion. Others and many tourists like the Tantalus view of Pearl Harbor, and Punchbowl, where the National Cemetery of the Pacific is located, but Chang liked the view from here better.

The view mo'bettah here. Plus, that when you at Punchbowl, get so too much tourists and you feel like there are so many others all around you. He just left it at that to himself. Next, he drove several miles to a major turn out to the Manoa Falls trail.

Reminds me of those small kid days when we just played and came up with our own games. None of this: "Hey you gotta go to soccer. Or no, how many times do I have to tell you, swimming lessons are every other Wednesday.

And how about all those piano or violin lessons. Hey, you have to practice if you want to win a scholarship. Otherwise you'll have to stay home and go to school here. Back then it was a mark of success: if you went to the mainland you were a success---both in high school and in the future. Well, BS to that, I said. It took him twenty minutes of a brisk hike to reach the scene of the picnic and death.

Ah, here's the spot.

He stepped gingerly over the yellow police tape, still dangling around the opening in the forest, where the unfortunate dead hiker met his maker. The trail ran straight through the almost round and flat area, where hikers often stopped to rest on nearby *ohia* tree logs to drink water and eat a snack. This part of the trail soon turned sharply towards a steep ridge, overlooking the upper part of Manoa valley. There were footprints all over the area in the mud. *Looks like all the evidence is messed up. Crime scene became a grime scene, he thought. I will leave the flora analysis to Moto, he thought. But there is just one plant I wonder about.*

There it is, the beautiful but sad Angels Trumpet. Carefully, with a pair of small kindergarten colored scissors, he snipped off two of its lily like flowers and eased them into a plastic bag. As a young boy, he was always warned that these droopy lilies were poison, but he needed to know more.

Chang was still unsatisfied. He had gone through the items the other police inspectors had found but he didn't find anything that was helpful.

Let's see. Though I'm older than those reunion grads and members of the Class of 94, I know they probably followed the same routine and same paths I did when I was in school. Hell, we all did. So, I don't want to believe everything they said about getting up here and then having a picnic. "Bullshit!" he roared, this time out loud. *It's a reunion. You want relive the past. So what did they do when they were younger and in college. Of course. They went to the old lookouts and they certainly must have smoked pot. I'm sure at least a couple of or three of them if not more, hell if not all them brought stuff with them. So let me see where were some of the favorite spots.*

Chang kept walking further and further from the original picnic site. He looked here and there but could not find anything interesting. He did realize that this was an energetic bunch. He found evidence of them from about quarter mile pass the picnic area. There were still bent folds of grass and broken bushes but nothing else in terms of evidence.

Chang kept roaming the different areas. He racked his brain, trying to think of all of the favorite spots of the past. Then he remembered. *Well there was this other place. It was my favorite and I liked to think that only I knew about it. Well maybe a few others did. Okay let me try there and then I'll go.*

After walking another ten minutes he came to a smaller clearing. And then: *Ha! It may not be them, but I bet you it was the fated 13. He had found some butts. Rich guys, they left some butts.* He put them away carefully. He decided to check some more and made a wide circle and then a still wider one. Under a bush he found still another butt. This was longer like the smoker decided to get rid of it sooner for some reason. He put that in a separate package and marked a nearby tree with a piece of red plastic tape, noting the exact location.

After a fifteen-minute walk back to his car, he carefully leaned the borrowed bamboo stick against a tree for the next hiker, and climbed into his DeLoreon, taking care not to muddy up his custom floor mats. Chang glided down Round Top Drive past the Manoa lookout, listening to his favorite version of an acid rock version of Vivaldi's Four Seasons. Winter was his favorite.

Well, it's time to go back down to Toronaga's, he was thinking to himself as he drove. This time, when he got to the base of Round Top Drive, he decided to go back through Manoa Valley, down Punahou Road and pass the famous private high school campus founded by missionaries, the home of two presidents of two different countries. *Everyone talks about Barack Obama. Yes, he went there and graduated, but people forget the Honorable Sun Yat Sen, the first President of modern day China. He went to Punahou, too.*

Okay, okay, the local guys who went to the two top schools here--- Punahou and Iolani---always argue over which school can claim him as their graduate since he attended both. Moto sides with the Iolani boys. Me, I go with the Buff and Blue.

Chang told himself it was just for laughs. *Main ting Hawaii had two Presidents and of the two economic giants of the world today. Any other place can claim that distinction? Naw.*

Wow, perfect time for lunch. At Moto's they must be on their break between the lunch crowd and before the dinner crowd.

CHAPTER 4

WITH A SONG IN MY HEART

June 2. 9am

Chang stopped for a moment before the door to the Office of Clare Song, the department's best crime scenes investigator. He chuckled to himself as he gave a hard but strangely melodic several knocks.

From behind the door there came a loud shout and a knock. "Oh come in Charlie. I know it's you. You're the only one with that knock".

"Ah my dear Ms. Song, you look ravishing today!"

"Oh bullshit Charlie. I was up all night and then I had to go out to fire they just put out because of suspected arson. I just came in and haven't even been able to wash up and all of the smudges and ashes and smears and"….Pausing, she went on, "And Charlie, you never knock unless you want a favor from me. So come on what is it? I'm really busy you know. I don't see how I can help you right away. You'll probably have to wait til next week. And that's only if I work through the weekend, you know."

"My dear Ms. Song, I only came here to give you some lunch. I know how busy you have been, and so I say to myself, poor Clare. She's probably working through lunch again. No time to go and get something to eat. Probably a staff member will have to get her some burger and fries, all of which will be cold and greasy by the time they get back to the station and make it to your office. And you know your Charlie…always thinking of you and your health and the need to keep up your good looks and figure," he said as he gives her the once over.

"Oh cut it out Charlie. I can only take so much bullshit from anyone, even you!"

"No, no, I mean that. Look! As he brings the small box he was hiding behind his back to place in front of her on the desk.

"Open. It's your very favorite, no can resist gyoza from Toronaga's. And it's your very special favorite---shrimp. I told Moto-san. Look, Clare is working so hard, before I start my lunch send one of your workers and get the very freshest shrimp from your dealer and come back and cook them for Ms. Song. Moto understood, and you know he thinks so highly of your work and skills, why even he stopped when the worker came back with get this, Live SHRIMP! And he took the shrimp and made the gyoza himself. Just for you. And I have your favorite - shoyu and mustard sauce with Moto's secret ingredients for the sauce he knows you love so much."

He opened the box and as harassed as she felt, Chang saw her eyes light up, and the smidgeon of a smile begin to appear.

"I told Moto, spare no expense. I pay for everything because Clare deserves. I'm the one person who truly appreciates her work and dedication and…"

"Oh cut it out Charlie. I know Moto always lets you eat for free. Everything is on the house. Plus, that you always get to take a doggy bag even though we both know you never leave anything on your plate. Oh excuse me----your plates---plural." But she was smiling now.

"I give in. What can I do for you, and only you?"

"I read your report on the evidence the staff investigators had brought back by surveying the picnic area for that unfortunate hike that cost one of the hikers his life. As you know, we believe along that he was a victim of foul play of some sort that led to poison in his system which did kill him. According to your report, there was nothing in the evidence or crime scene objects that gives any light on the poor Mr. Flores' death. Did I miss anything Clare?"

"Yes and No. No, you're certainly right I could not find anything. For all I know, the so called evidence might not have even belonged to any member of the party. I understand the spot is pretty popular, or it was at one time. But people hike everywhere now, so I would not be surprised that the items might have been from previous groups or individuals who were hiking or who chose to picnic there. The photos

I saw make it look like a great place to have a small picnic party. Who knows, maybe I'll go up there one day. I'll save your next box of gyoza for an early pau hana dinner. Ha, ha, ha!" She laughed.

"Ok. That's the No. What's the *yes* of it?"

Song became very serious. "It's the state of the body. Clearly the poison affected his entire system. There was evidence of paralysis of smooth muscles, tachycardia, dry mouth, diarrhea, mydriasis, rapid onset cycloplegia – all leading to a painful death. Had he lived longer, there might have been all kinds of painful lead-ups to his demise."

"Oh, now you are waaay over this humble Chang's head with the medical terms. But can I assume you have a suspicion about what the actual cause was?"

"Possibly. Tentatively. I have read articles about the attractive yet highly poisonous drooping lilly tree called Angels' Trumpet. Turns out there is quite a range of toxicity, especially its flower and seeds. Depends, in part, on the subspecies, and where it grows. Usually, it takes a day or two for the more intense systemic impacts, and sometimes it might look like a heart attack. But there are cases where mortality can come quickly. Unfortunately, traces of it tend to dissipate quickly. So while there is some evidence…can't be absolutely sure."

"Well, Ms. Clare, I decided to go up there myself. I quickly scanned the picnic site where the inspectors concentrated their effort. But I went well beyond that scope. I found some other items. True, there might have been left by hikers who had been there previously. I think, with the crime scene ribbons, it's unlikely though, but still possible for others to have come by in the past five days. I left with several small bags. A couple are half smoked joints. Maybe keep on hand if we need to match up DNA later. At the very least, they paint a picture of a group not adverse to using some drugs, even if it may be technically illegal. But the important ones are these."

Clare Song picked up the flower bags and smiled. Each bag clearly held an Angel's Trumpet flower, one pink, one white.

"Now Clare. Keep them separate. The white one was growing near the picnic site. The pink from another area of the trail leading to it."

"OK, I will test both and see if they match up in type and intensity of the toxins I found in the Flores body. But I would caution that whether they do or not, might not mean anything. It would only be relevant IF, and this is a big IF, somehow Flores ingested the poison at that site, and from that plant."

"Yes, understood," said Chang, admiring her thoroughness.

"Yes, and there is one more thing. Could be important, but certainly not relating to the immediate death."

"What's that?"

"Mr. Flores was also suffering from an advanced stage of liver cancer. Probably had no more than six months to live."

C H A P T E R   5

MY POOR YELLOW DATSUN-SAN

June 2. 11 am

"Come on old car, you can make it up Round Top Drive one more time. Come on, don't make Moto abandon you on the lookout near the so-called *hogsback*, waiting for surfing kids to strip you of your usable parts." Moto punched the clutch and took the turn near the park entrance as wide as he could, since no cars were coming down.

Chang wanted a second opinion before we meet about case, so it's you an me, Yellow buddy. "Moto, I need your eyes. You see differently. You understand what you see differently. And you know the rainforest better than I do," Chang said. Moto appreciate being appreciated.

Moto enjoyed his frequent hikes in the rainforest. It was his way of relieving the stress of running a popular restaurant. He avoided Tantalus on Wednesday's and Sundays, as that's when the pig hunters, with their frisky and vicious dogs, were allowed to hunt the wild boars in the hills.

Today's hike was with purpose, not just to enjoy the smells and sights, to relax his mind to think.

Moto eased into the muddy parking area near the main trail to Manoa Falls. *Ah, good, friendly hikers left bamboo walking sticks for next visitor to rain forest. Nice tradition. Nice Aloha for someone you don't even know.*

Moto was a student of Hawaii's natural environment. He made it a point of reading up on the plants and animals before his frequent hikes.

Moto love this hike through the tall bamboo. Love the sound of the wind and the creaking, swaying, aching bamboo trees. Remind Moto of Kyoto. Ah, here the spot.

Moto saw the yellow police tape. He continued down the trail where it veered toward a steep ridge. Yoshiro, "Moto" Fujimoto, Japanese restaurant owner, and part time silent detective friend and partner of Inspector Charlie C. Chang, began a thorough review of the surrounding areas. He walked into the bamboo thickets and took note of the plants, the trees, the smells, the groundcover. He pulled a small, worn notebook from his back pocket and began scribbling in Japanese with a stubby pencil. His notes were in Kanji, Japanese modified Chinese characters. *One kanji worth ten thousand words,* he often told Chang.

His eye caught something. *Ah, good fortune to see this,* he thought. He stooped and examined several broken branches, and the nearby distinctive shoe prints in the mud. Where the trail overlooked the scenic Manoa valley – home of the University of Hawaii – his attention was on the invasive albesia trees way down in the valley. He tried not to look at the nondescript UH buildings which he considered an eyesore, except for the really older ones, and the Chosen Dynasty replica Korean Studies Center, which he regarded as the best building on campus.

Now Moto go high tech, heh, heh. From his blue and white palaka shirt pocket, the one he bought at the old Arakawa's general store in Waipahu before it closed, out came a smart phone. He retraced his steps stopping often to take digital pictures of the terrain and anything else that caught his eye. *Chang think Moto live in Samurai time with nothing but pencil and pad. Moto surprise him one day, heh, heh.* He liked to wear his palaka shirt, for it reminded him of the immigrants who came to work the sugar and pineapple plantations. For some reason, this table cloth like pattern had first come with sailors, but its durability transferred easily to the field workers. He too, took note of the Angel's Trumpet. He timed how long it took to walk from the main picnic spot in the bamboo grove to the lookout. It was farther than he expected. Four minutes. *And this is supposedly where Mr. Flores met his fate.* He could see in the mud how his classmates had dragged the body back to the picnic spot. He made a few more notes, and shoved the pad back into his pocket.

He decided to take a slightly different route back down to the parking lot. He was particularly heading for a cement bench overlooking Manoa. He wanted to spend a few minutes in slow breathing - meditation.

He came to the bench. *Funny, Moto never notice this before. Not bad for amateur kadomatsu. Used good sharp saw. Why placed here?* He wondered.

It was fairly fresh, with the outer bamboo still green. He peered over the edge of the ridge. Not five feet away he could see an older version, no doubt blown over by a storm. Its outer parts tan, and covered with the mold that grew on everything in an environment that got more than 100 inches of rain a year.

He looked closer. The straw rope knots were poorly done. *Artist know how cut bamboo, but not how to tie rope. Not professional. Personal. Why here?*

Carefully, gingerly, he edged his way over the steep side of the trail and was just able to grab the top of the older "gate pine."

He examined it closely. Same saw. Same knots. Although two feet tall, it was not heavy. Age had thinned and lightened the stalks.

Better get banana car going back down. Prepare lunch. After a fifteenminute walk back to the muddy parking lot, he carefully leaned the borrowed bamboo stick against a tree for the next hiker, and climbed into his unlocked car. *Any crazy person want to steal you, Datsun-san, be my guest,* he laughed to himself. With good fortune, and no car trouble, Moto glided down Round Top past the Manoa lookout, listening to an old tape of slack key guitar legend Gabby Pahinui…*No make em like Gabby no more…*

C H A P T E R 6
THE NETWORK

June 3

Three o'clock. Moto looked at his watch. He reflected to himself. *That was a hectic lunch; now a short break and I can relax.* A loud car came sounding through the windows and walls of Toronaga's.

Well so much for a break. It can only be Chang-san. A loud blast from the car sounded and then the engine was killed.

Chang came bursting through the entrance, "Hey Moto!' he shouted as he came to Moto's table.

"Charlie-san why you have to gun your De Lorean when you've already come to a stop."

"Hey! It's just to let folks know I'm here. You know, so they can get ready."

"But Charlie, your De Lorean makes so much noise you can hear it a block away. You sure car legal?"

"Now Moto, we've been through this before. You are looking at Honolulu's finest. Do you think I would openly flaunt the law? I've never gotten a ticket in my life. Well, if you overlook the uku-millions when I was a kid. I didn't know I'd become a cop."

Moto had heard that story before and prayed that Charlie would not repeat it.

"Well, I came cause of the new case we've been pondering. I wanted to pick your brains. It's a stomper." As he said that a waitress came up to the table.

"Oh, sir, Mr. Moto does not permit people to come here during his break."

Moto cut in. "Carol, I know, in the briefing I gave you the rules about who gets to sit with me or gets to use the table. And it true, that during break between lunch and dinner, only I sit here. But there is one exception. I should have explained. And here's the exception. Honorable Charlie Chang, one of Honolulu's finest."

Moto could see how red faced she became. But it was his fault in not briefing the new hire.

"In that case sir, what would you like to order."

Moto was impressed with her speedy recovery. *Good manners and reflexes*, he thought.

Charlie made his order. "I usually say the usual, and in fact most already know what I want, but you're new so"… he proceeded to order. "And don't mind the face the boss is making, he's always like that. I always tell him, but for me it's a light lunch! She took it down with a smile, and turned to enter the kitchen.

"Moto, I emailed you about the death of the hiker on Tantalus last Saturday. I went up there and I understand you did too. I appreciate you looking at the same places, the same clues, and coming up with an out of the box interpretation." Without waiting, he went on. "It wasn't a heart attack or stroke or some kind of fall or exhaustion. It appears to be murder. He was poisoned. Report and chemical analysis are all here. I spoke to Clare. We both suspect Angles' Trumpet. I made a copy for you. But keep to yourself. Give it back after we've solved the case, as usual, Moto."

"Did you get a chance to go for a nice hike?" asked Charlie with a twinkle in his eye.

"Moto hiked, took notes, tell you later when think about it."

Moto pulled out some of the papers from the file. It included a photo of a group of hikers and their names. Each had a brief description.

All the while, Chang kept talking. "The victim is Ben Flores. That's him there." Chang pointed to one of the faces in the crowd. "Of the remaining twelve, some live here, others on the mainland. But they're all classmates and Grover Cleveland High School buddies. Their class had their 20th reunion last week. Original class of '94. These thirteen decided to stay longer and catch up on events. They were all going to hang for a week or so. One of the ideas was to go hiking up on Manoa Cliffs, up there on Tantalus. You've been there, Moto? I t was a big gathering place back in college."

"Moto heard some old time hippies were growing pot a couple of decades back in a nearby meadow."

Chang continued. "I don't know any of them, but the Chair of the Police Commission personally asked that I handle the investigation. I even met with him and the Chief to get the assignment. This has never happened to me before. That's why I thought I should get your thoughts first. I don't know any of them, and I have yet to talk to them."

Moto interrupted." I have seen some of them. Not as group - wakarimasu, but see several, including poor murder victim before."

"Now, Moto", Chang exclaimed, "how can you remember those faces? Some don't even live in Hawaii anymore. And you weren't around when they were in high school."

"I tell you before Charlie-san, I nevah forget a face. Any face. Specially guests here at restaurant. But other than that, I don't know names. Some have been here several times, but they were probably someone else's guest. I would know the name of the person who put together dinner party, but that all."

"Well, look at the file. You'll find their names and a little bio. I will be interviewing them, of course, and appointments are being set up as we sit here. You know Moto, I gotta know something about your memory. Yeah I know you got a photographic memory."

"What you like know Charlie? Seems you must have some kind of memory like that. You no forget anything."

"Well, Moto, here's what I want to know. Before the camera was invented what did they call your kind of memory of faces, scenes, the trees in the forest, the colors of this and that. I mean did they say you had a Rembrandt memory because everybody looked like a Rembrandt painting? Or you had a Hieronymus Bosch memory because everyone looked one his paintings instead? And Moto, here's what I really want to know. What kind of camera is it?

"What you mean Charlie? You mean like I got Kodak or Nikon? Or…" *How Charlie know I get smart phone?*

"No Moto, I mean after the digital camera was invented, does your memory use film photography or is it digital? Do you have a roll of film or a chip inside that crazy head? And yes, I happen to know you have a Samsung Galaxy 5 smart phone. Don't look shocked. I keep track of all the seedy characters in our town." Chang then started to laugh as the waitress returned with his steaming order. She needed the whole tray.

Moto know Charlie suspect different thinking. Long time since doctors told parents – Okaasan, Otoosan, your boy has a special gift. He's is normal mostly, but his ability to focus and remember, kind of savant like. He'll always be different, but not in a bad way, he said.

He ate, they chatted. Then Charlie looked at his Rolex and excused himself.

Moto spent some time looking at the pictures, and had previously used his computer to access links to the Facebook pages many had, and which the police IT division had found. and began to think about the 13. Moto shuffled off to his office in the back of the restaurant, enjoying the sizzling smell of the Osaka style okonomiyaki pancake. He pulled his thin laptop from the drawer and booted it up. For each picture and short bio, including access to links to the Facebook pages many had, and which the police IT division had found. He took notes, all in Japanese sprinkled with kanji. It was his way of ensuring most nosy people would not easily know what he was writing.

Victim. Ben Flores. Lived in Kailua. Cleveland High grad. Multiple arrests for drug possession. Has worked as a waiter in Waikiki. Recently was an *Uber* driver.

All survivors Cleveland High School grads, just down the hill from Round Top and Tantalus. Probably all knew the rain forest, the trails, maybe the plants…All 38 years old, or there abouts. Six males, seven females. Start with women.

Sarah Taira, Wendy Gushiken, Maya Kai, Shirley Garcia, Eileen Kerrigan, Judy Conlin. Wait, this Maya girl, wasn't she eating here with our stellar reporter girl Zoe Lee? Maybe call Zoe later. Ok, personal lives.

Sarah Taira – lives in Punchbowl condo; married with one daughter, divorced, went to law school here, practices criminal law with smallish firm.

Wendy Gushiken – lives in Manoa, married, two young kids, is a chef at the Pacific Club, husband is a banker of some sort. Charlie say Chief Commissioner show lot of interest in this wahine.

Maya Kai, lives in Waipahu, bounced around working in hotels, owns a small accounting firm, single.

Judy Conlin – lives in Helena Montana, runs outdoor adventure tours; single.

Shirley Garcia – lives in Kalihi; works as a physical therapist at the Rehab Hospital; married to a dental hygienist; no children.

Shirley Garcia – lives in Kalihi; works as a physical therapist at the Rehab Hospital; married to a dental hygienist; no children.

Eileen Kerrigan – lives in New York. Does IT for Lemoyne College.

Ok, Moto see professionals – teacher, lawyer, chef, small business owner…All smaht wahine.

Now the men.

Gary Hoe – lives in Waianae; teaches math at Leeward Community College; married, wife manages golf shop at Kapolei golf course; three young boys.

Reed Radcliff – lives in San Francisco; investment advisor for futures stocks; married co-worker at same firm; adopted a baby girl from China.

William Kalaiopula - lives in Makiki, works for State Department of Land and Natural Resources, manages forest reserve program. Never married.

Jake Kim – lives in Hawaii Kai, Pharmacist at HealthRite Drug Store; married to preschool teacher; two young children.

Jarrett Tanji – Lives in Pearl City, used car salesman; divorced. Supports ex-wife and daughter.

Jason Menor – Lives in Los Angeles, plays soccer for the LA Galaxy. Married to fashion designer. Two sons.

Moto see some interesting patterns. Who knows about poison?

Sarah Taira – knows criminal law. Could she know how to poison a victim?

Wendy Gishiken – a chef. Maybe know what not to eat.

William Kalaiopula – know forest, know plants.

Jake Kim – druggist – bingo? Not too much but some ideas. Need know connections, networks, relationships….

C H A P T E R   7
A NOT SO ROUTINE ARTICLE

June 3

Zoe Lee was not happy about being asked to do what she considered a typical small time crime story. She was deep into her research on an emerging social crisis – spreading throughout suburban America, including Hawaii. The rapid growth of prescription drug dependency and abuse was very much a part of a cluster of issues, including heroin and crystal meth. She hated to be yanked away from a total-immersion investigation. A high school reunion had gone sour, and one man had died, apparently from poison. It might be an accident; it might be foul play. *Any number of other reporters should be doing this*, she thought. She soon discovered it was a story worth probing. A friend of hers who was in the same hula halau was part of that reunion.

"Maya, you look kind of upset today," Zoe observed after practice.

"Zoe, you wouldn't believe what happened. Our 20th high school class reunion was on a hike up on Tantalus, and one of the guys died right in front of us, screaming, in pain."

"Funny you should mention that. I was just assigned to write a short article about it. What do you know?"

"It's a long story, but this is not the first time something like this has happened."

"What do you mean?"

"Ten years ago, almost to the day, we had our first reunion. We also took a hike, and, man, it still upsets me to think about it. A girl fell off the trail and died."

"Two reunions and two deaths? That's some coincidence. Do you think they are connected?"

"I don't know what to think. But some detective has been calling and asking to interview most of us about this year's death."

It did not take Zoe Lee, award winning reporter for the on-line Manoa Investigator, to find out more, and put together a short. *This is worth following up on later,* she thought. She first looked up Maya's social media pages, which included a whole cluster of pictures of former classmates. She also made a discrete phone call to her friend, Moto.

THE MANOA INVESTIGATOR

June 3, 2014

by Zoe Lee

Police are investigating a suspicious death in the Tantalus rainforest, above Honolulu. On May 30, while on a 20th Cleveland High School reunion, 38-year-old Benjamin Flores died a painful death. Fellow hikers reported that Flores collapsed following shrieks of pain. They were able to haul his unresponsive body to their cars. He was pronounced dead upon arrival at Hawaii Prince Hospital. Police are investigating the possibility of foul play.

C H A P T E R   8
RINGGG
June 3

Zoe Calls Moto

Ringgg!

"Hai. Zoe-san. Good to hear from you. You like some good sushi, Zoe? Saving for you, you know. What, you tink Moto get ace up sleeve, hidden agenda? Hai. Ok, Ok. What can Moto do for you? You know one of those ladies in the Tantalus reunion group, yeah? Wasser name? Maya. Right. So she kind of auntie to you yeah? You guys do hula together. Here what Moto want to know. Need more background on class members. Maybe you… What? No kid Moto, now Zoe-san. Ten years before another reunion. Same group. Same place, rain forest? One girl fall off trail and die. Name Sabrina something? Matsumoto. Maya told you? What about old archives, do papers still keep? You look, right? Find out anything, the sushi is on Moto."

Click.

Moto Calls Chang

Ringgg!

"Chang here. Yes, Moto. You sound like you found something. Oh, Zoe Lee found something. You've got to be kidding. Another suspicious death? Ten years ago? OK, what was her name again? Yes, I'm at my computer now. Let me open up that older data base. Just take a minute. Wait. 2004. OK, here it is. Let me do the search. OK. Yes. Sabrina Matsumoto. Apparently fell off the trail, some 40 feet. Died at the scene. Officially recorded as an accidental death. Wow, looks like we interviewed a few hikers, and, yes, as you suspected. Same names as on the Flores case. Oh, this is rich. This is sooo rich. No, Moto, Flores was not rich, but this other information is extremely interesting. Our records give the address she was living at back then. I'll give you one guess, and a hint. It was in Kakaako. Bingo. Yes, unbelievable. She actually rented a room from our favorite landlords – Joseph and Molly Davis. Yeah, they one's we call the Mai Tai's cuz they always bring their own to watch the sunsets. But you think this is somehow related to the Flores case? Just your gut, huh? Maybe we should try to find out about this same group back in 2004. You want to do it? Got time? Oh, yes, I see what you mean. Japanese family, would talk to official authority, like me, but not scruffy guy like you? Yes, I think it might be worth the time. Tell you what. You reach out to the Mai Tai's, I see if I can get in touch with the Matsumotos."

Moto Calls the Mai Tais

Ringgg!

"This Joe Davis? This Moto, remember me? No use foul language. Not called for, Mr. Mai Tai, guess you don't want your free prize. You been selected, Kakaako landlord of year. Hai. Yes. Fo real. Chamber of Commerce choose. OK. Put on wife. Molly, this Moto. Hey, mimiga itai…make Moto ears hurt. Be nice, got free five-course dinner for you and your charming husbin. Hai. Don't ask Moto. Not my choice. But Chamber guys pick Moto high-class restaurant for prize. Only problem, got to collect your free meal in one week. Can? No Can? What. Tonite? Hey, you think we keep table just for you?"

"Hey you tink we dumb haoles? There's no award. What do you really want?"

"Oh, Moto cannot fool you guys. Actually, want to meet. Show you something. You be under that banyan tree at Magic Island usual time? Good. See you then."

Click.

Moto think this poison case turning into one Aggie Christie type convoluted web. One group, two reunions. Both in forest. Two dead. One murder for sure. Don't get ahead of self, Moto. Maybe connected, maybe not. Nothing more crazy than high school classmates...

* * *

Chang Calls Sabrina's Parents

Ringgg!

"Hello, Mrs. Matsumoto? This is Detective Charlie C. Chang of the Honolulu Police Department. I'm not sure if we ever met ten years ago when you lost your daughter. I am so sorry. And so sorry to bring up what must be a painful memory. Well, Ok I'll wait. Yes, Mr. Matsumoto, I'm glad you are both on the phone. The reason for my call is that another case has come up that involves some of your daughter's classmates, and I was wondering if I might stop by and ask you a few questions. Yes. Yes. Precisely. No, we have nothing to report to you. Yes, I know you always thought there was something more to her death than a sudden accident. No, as I said, we don't have anything more. Well, the reason is that we wanted to ask you about Sabrina's relationships, and anything, anything at all you might know about that reunion and her classmates. Yes, that's right. About a dozen I think. Yes, OK, that would be great if you could dig out that yearbook, maybe jar some memories. Yes. How about Saturday morning, will you be home? About ten? Yes. I really appreciate it. Yes. Thank you for your willingness to speak to me. Aloha."

Click.

Sen. Watanabe Calls Chang

Ringgg!

"Detective Chang here. Yes, Senator Watanabe. How have you been? May I thank you again for your generous gift to the Police Benevolent Fund. Yes, all the officers are aware of your contribution. Yes, we printed it in the annual report, just like we promised. Yes. May I ask what is the reason for your call? Yes, I understand you represent the upper Makiki / Tantalus district. Yes, well I really can't say anything more than what was on the news. Yes, I understand that the residents are upset. No, I would not say that crime is out of control. I would say, actually, it is down the last three years. Yes, I understand. Sure, I can send one of our officers to brief the residents at their next meeting. Now, Senator, you are mentioning a specific name, and specific alleged crime. You know I can't talk about it in any detail. You think you have a suspect, do you? Look, Senator, may I respectfully suggest that it is time for the police to do their work. I'm sure in good time we will meet with you and hear what you have to say. Yes, yes, I promise…in good time…as I said…Thank you for service and your interest in your community. We always appreciate it. Yes. Thank You.

Click.

Whiskey – Tango – Foxtrot. What a dork. Seems to have an awfully big interest in this case. Course, always wanting to look good to the voters… but something else. A little too intense. A little too informed. Need to have staff dig around in the Senator's background if he gets too nosey.

C H A P T E R   9
OKONOMIYAKI TALK

June 4. 11 am

Through the slit in the *noren* Moto grinned as he saw Zoe Lee, award winning investigative reporter for *The Manoa*, an on-line news organization. He got to know her two years earlier when her fiancée was murdered, and she showed her grit and her professionalism in helping Moto and Chang solve the case. She was with a slightly older, part-Hawaiian woman, who Moto knew to be Maya Kai, one of the Tantalus reunion group. He waited for them to order her favorite Japanese style pancake – Osaka style okonmiyaki. They beamed when a complementary ceramic dispenser of hot sake arrived.

Moto see these two wahine have good friendship. They smile, they laugh, they finish each other's' sentences.

Moto made the rounds to the various tables, delighting the guests with his attention. Zoe was pleasantly surprised when Moto sat down at their table and introduced himself.

"Good to see Zoe-san again. You look good girl. Bouncing back, Moto think," he said, always referring to himself in the third person. Zoe would kid him about trying to imitate Mr. Miyagi from the Karate Kid movies. "What you talk about? Moto not see movie. Moto is Moto, period."

"Moto, I'd like to introduce my friend Maya. We met in our hula halau, and have spent a lot of time together, as our group was chosen for competition. Maya, I have to confess. This is not strictly a social dinner. Oh, I love to eat here and bring my friends, but I especially wanted to introduce you to the owner of the best Izakaya in Honolulu, and its semi-detective, Moto."

"Moto glad to meet Maya. How you like the sake? Special dry style. Different, yeah?"

Maya nodded, not sure what to make of this older man with a salt and pepper goatee. "I love it. Mahalo for the treat. Zoe, you sure have some interesting contacts in this town. I grew up here, like you, but you really are connected!"

Zoe nodded, but her mouth was full of pancake filled with cabbage and crabs, smothered in Japanese mayo.

"So sorry to interrupt your dinner, but Moto have some questions like to ask, OK? Well, wondering about this tragic incident up Tantalus, school friend die, die too young, just late 30s. And Moto also wondering about that last reunion, ten years ago."

"You mean Sabrina Matsumoto?"

"Hai. You close with Sabrina?" Maybe you know if she had boyfriend?"

"First of all, I am freaked out that in two reunions we have two deaths. What are the odds? It's spooky, ya know? First Sabrina falls off the trail, now Ben....."

"Moto ask about boyfriend."

"Hmmm. Let me think," said Maya. "Come to think of it, I think she was seeing someone, a classmate. But it is kind of awkward. See, her, friend, was married."

"Moto understand. Moto discrete, but need to know. Name please."

"It was Jake. Jake Kim. But puleeze. No need to complicate Jake's marriage. He's a pharmacist, and is married with one or two kids. And that was over ten years ago. No need messing up their lives."

"So Sabrina had relationship with Jake. What relationship with Ben Flores?"

"Ben, pardon me from sayin, but someone who was always in trouble. Some said he did drugs. Some said he sold drugs."

"Maya," broke in Zoe. "You can trust Moto. He is trying to understand relationships and what happened. Don't feel you need to hold back. Take it from me, I know from experience."

Maya looked at Zoe, searching her face and eyes for reassurance. Zoe had, over an emotional late night drink, filled Maya in on the relationship Zoe developed with Moto and Inspector Charlie Chang. Both intertwined with the death of Zoe's boyfriend. It was painful, and Maya was not quite comfortable to see this confident and smart young reporter sobbing uncontrollably. After that, they became close friends.

"OK. Here is what I know, or think I know. Ben and Sabrina had a thing in high school, but it didn't go anywhere. At least not for a while. Later, and I don't know how it happened, but they met at a beach on the North Shore, and things got chummy. More than that, Ben gave her drugs. I think it might have been meth, but I'm not sure. After that, Sabrina seemed to be drifting away from the high school grads. We might get together sometimes at Zippy's Diner, but Sabrina was never around. Didn't answer her phone. We felt Ben was slowly dragging her into his world. Someone said she was even sleeping around. Maybe had an abortion. Hard on her folks, really traditional Japanese, you know. But just rumors. Anyway, she somehow got it into her head that she wanted Jake. Maybe it was a way of getting away from Ben. At first, Jake resisted. Happily married, yada yada. But she was persistent. And she was a good looking chick. Took care of herself. Kept slim. Wore low cut tops. Jake never had a chance."

"Moto appreciate this information. Who else know about Sabrina and Jake? Wife know? Others?"

"A few of us knew, but you know that was over ten years ago, back in 2002. I'm not sure anymore. Just something that was out there, you know? And then when Sabrina died, it all seemed unimportant. In spite of her lifestyle, she was still our good friend. Our classmate."

Zoe could see that the conversation was upsetting Maya. "Moto, maybe we have covered this enough for now?"

"Moto sorry, spoil meal. Too nosy. Enjoy dinner. Please forgive. Moto busy in office. Mahalo."

"Maya, I'm so sorry. Didn't know it would get this intense. Let's talk about something else, OK?"

"K," said Maya, who clearly had lost her appetite.

C H A P T E R   1 0
DETECTIVE WORK CAN BE TEDIOUS

June 4

Chang was just driving around. He did that to clear his thinking. He had just had lunch at Moto's place and then when he returned to the station. It was his practice to review the facts of each case once in the morning, when his mind was fresh, and once more in the late afternoon or night. It was his personal belief that insights and patterns revealed themselves at different times or in different moods. Yet the workload, and this new case, were making him a very busy detective. He laughed to himself remembering yet another brief encounter with the Chief.

The Chief had poked his head in Charlie's office. "How are we doing on the hiker case?"

"Everything in good time, Chief. You wanted me to meet with the Police Commissioner Chair. And from that meeting came the new case. And you know not just any new case but one that comes from the Commission and from its Chairman There are only so many hours in a day. Straight from that meeting up to view the crime scene. You gotta hike in, on top of that, and I am not as young as I used to be, you know. And that goes for the two of us."

The Chief wore a Cheshire cat smile on his face. He had been through these mild protests of Chang's for years. It had become a game between the two of them. The Chief would play the role of supervisor, chiding, prodding. Yet he knew that Charlie was on top of every case, and usually way ahead in his analysis.

"Now Charlie, I know you took a two hour lunch at Toronaga's. and don't dodge it. A couple of police cars saw your infamous De Lorean parked a short distance from the restaurant in a no parking zone. And since they were rookie cops they called in and wondered if they should ticket the famous Charlie Chang. They all know your car, but the new guys have to be broken in, you know. So the beat captain said no, because you were probably on a case. Otherwise he told them you always follow the parking regs." Of course this was all a lie, and he knew that Charlie knew it too.

"And Chang, I did overhear you telling the new secretary about your weekend surfing and how you've also been training for the Honolulu Marathon. I believe the surfing part but you haven't run the Marathon in ten years, Chang. But she believed both stories. So don't tell me you struggled gung ho up that hill and it is a hill not a mountain. I've been up there!"

Charlie laughed to himself as he kept driving. He did finish reviewing the reports and wanted to clear his mind. He went down to his favorite spot near the yacht club, tucked into a parking stall, and walked to his favorite stone wall and just sat. He was thinking about the first interviews he had with hikers on that fateful trek up to the bamboo grove. He met with them one at a time and, as usual, sized them up, as well as got their versions of the events of that fateful day.

The first person he chose to see had been Reed Radcliff. He was one of those who now lived on the mainland, and Chang thought it best that he should interview the mainlanders first. They had all been asked to stay until the investigation was over. Most had plans to stay a week longer, since they had not been back for years. All were cooperative. It was, it seems, a close knit group. They all wanted to know what had happened to their "small keed" friend and classmate.

Reed was staying at one of the best hotels in Waikiki. Chang especially liked the place because they had one of his favorite coffee shops in the complex. He had phoned earlier and asked that Reed meet him there. Chang was sitting at one of the tables ahead of Reed's entrance.

"Hi! I'm Reed Radcliff."

"Oh yes, Mr. Reed! the cashier-waitress said. He had eaten many of his meals here. "Always good to see you!" Although he'd only been a hotel guest for a week, Reed was already known as a very generous tipper. "Your usual table?'

"Not this time, Nani. I'm here to see Inspector Chang. He said to ask you where I could find him. I guess he's a regular here too."

"Oh, he comes often enough. He is always flirting with the younger waitresses, promising to take them to Maui for a weekend. Plus, you know he's very famous. They say he always gets his man or his woman. And there was that strange case where he got that awful kid."

"So, Mr. Chang is already here and just to tell you where his favorite table is. He's out there on the lanai, table is on the right when you get out. You can't mistake him, because he's the only one occupying a table right now."

Reed went out to the lanai, turned right and he saw the gentlemen sitting on that second table nearest the beach side. He was facing away from the beach though. Reed would have sat facing the beach. Women in the tightest swim suits were already out soaking in the sun. Chang was already having tea.

As he approached, the inspector got up and said. "You must be Reed. Thank you for coming. Please sit down. Please don't mind me for starting soon. I saved the best seat on the table for you." He said with a smile.

"You know people come from all over the world to see the ocean and waves and the great sandy beach here in Waikiki. I know you grew up here, - but - if you're like me you can never get enough of the sand and surf and everything that goes with it," he said with a smile.

"That's so true, Inspector Chang. San Francisco's a great city and there's so much there that I wish we had here, but Waikiki is still incomparable, even though there are so many more tourists than when I was growing up in the 80's."

"How true," Chang said. "Sorry, but I just started. Didn't have breakfast at home. And then I just love chef's pancakes. Oh, and the burnt like crispy bacon! But go ahead and order anything. Chef said the blueberries just came in yesterday."

"No, I'll have something else. And you're right, Chef Nakamura is great. He said he's from the Kapiolani Community College culinary arts program. Their grads have beaten some of the top culinary schools in the nation, you know." Reed felt initially at ease with Chang, but behind the friendly façade, there was a seriousness, a no nonsense look in his eyes. "But you know, I've been here for over a week now and I haven't had a single bowl of Loco Moco. So I hope you don't mind."

"Please," Chang said. He felt that Reed was more comfortable now, talking to an investigator. You made a great choice. Nakamura's Loco Moco is one of the best. You know when you live here you can never say any one person's Loco Moco is THE BEST. You would lose a lot of friends and family that way. Folks take it real seriously, as I'm sure you know."

Reed nodded as he made his order for the Loco Moco with extra gravy.

"Reed, while we're waiting for your order, tell me what happened up there from the time you were picked up. I understand the thirteen of you squeezed into three cars. And I've already read what's in the filed police reports and they included your brief bios. If I need anything more information on your background, I'll ask before leaving today."

Reed's demeanor and expression turned morose. "I still can't believe it. Two reunions and two deaths! Ten years ago one of our group, Sabrina, fell off the trail. Took three hours with the helicopter and everything to get her body. We were all so bummed out, we just skipped the 15th reunion. So now for the second time. It's unbelievable. Really."

Chang was scribbling notes. "So there was another death ten years ago?" Chang often pretended he didn't know what he knew. "We need to talk about that too. But getting back to this year, this tragedy."

"Well, it was agreed ahead of time that Gary and Jake would bring their SUVs. Maya took her van. They would pick us up at home or at our hotel at specified times. I got in with Jake. We wanted to take as few cars as possible up there because as you know Mr. Chang, it's always hard to find parking. And your car is always at risk. Jake and Gary had the most protected cars with all sorts of alarms. Of course where we were going, who could hear them? And it was like old times cause even back then Jake and Gary had the biggest cars. Not necessarily the best cars. In fact, I think they had the oldest ones. But they liked working on them. Gary used to do a little drag racing in high school, and his car was not quite street legal you know." Chang made an ever so slight chuckle when he heard that. He immediately felt a kinship to Gary whom he had yet to meet.

"So I got picked up here and since I was the last of the bunch Gary picked up, we took off to Tantalus."

"Just a slight interruption, Reed. Who was in your car?" Chang asked.

"Well, let's see. Gary drove. There was Jarrett Tanji, Jason Menor, Judy Conlin, and me.

"Chang interrupted, "I assume the two ladies were also staying in hotels since they're from the mainland."

"No, they stayed with their parents who have some fancy condos in the Kakaako area. Boy, has that area changed from car repair shops and lunch places and bars to mega-millionaires' vacations condos. Their folks are okay, but not rich. They lucked out and got into the few senior affordable living apartments when that was the goal of the state public housing people. That's all changed now, I see. Money talks to politicians." Chang nodded, as to keep him on track.

"So we went to the top of the mountain. Of course you know we made the usual stops at the Manoa side look out and of course at Puu Ualakaa park and the lookout there. I think we stayed at the park for about 45 minutes to an hour, as I recall. Then we went to the hogsback. Lucked into parking, and we started that steep hike up the maintenance road for the utilities. We got to the bamboo grove and walked for, I'd say, ten to fifteen minutes. We made it to the meadow near the thick bamboo trail. You've been there, right? Or at least you know whereabouts I'm speaking."

"Yes, I know. I took a short hike up there when I checked out the police report. There's still police tape all over or around the spots you folks stayed."

"Well, we all sat down in the shaded area. It was still about 2 o' clock. The sun was high enough and a little hot and burning. It would need another hour to begin tapering off. But, of course, with all the trees and tall bamboo, it was manageable. We all sat together. And we talked story, and remembered about old days. Some had pictures of their kids. I had adopted a girl from China three years before, so I was proudly showing Brooke's pictures, especially of her at her preschool pageant. A couple of the girls might have walked off to check out some favorite sites which were nearby. Probably remembering some special afternoon, you know?"

Chang let him ramble, holding back his impatience. Hoping for some useful information.

"Ben was getting a little loud as I recall. I couldn't quite hear what he was complaining about. He was mainly with Wendy, Sarah, Bill, Gary and Jake. We had a couple or three small groups within the group."

"It was mid-afternoon and we were hungry and thirsty, so we broke out the bentos, the sushi rolls, the drinks, the beer, oh, maybe I shouldn't say that. Our knapsacks were filled with goodies. We even had hot tea in thermoses."

"Hot tea, you say."

"Then, I think it was Will's idea. He yelled out. Hey remember when you girls used to dance the hula in high school. Don't tell you folks have forgotten how to dance the hula. Like bicycle riding, you supposed to never forget how."

"Soon all of us, well, all the guys, were shouting out and began clapping in unison for the girls to dance. They were all red in the face but then Maya said, "Okay you asked for it. And you're gonna get it. Maya is actually still active in a halau. So she took charge. They were all laughing now."

"The girls all went off to side about 20 feet away. They began to confer among themselves. I guess they were choosing a number. Then there some kind of agreement and they were making a few practice motions. Then they all came out. Maya, no it was Wendy who shouted out a name of a hula number."

"Now, I should say, Will in our gang was a terrific ukulele player. He never went anywhere without his uke. So he had taken it with him, and brought up to the trail. So Wendy had shouted to Will to play a song. And they started dancing. We were all yelling and shouting and clapping. It was like old times again. Those girls could dance!"

"Some of us yelled "Hana Ho" Hana Ho! to encourage an encore. The girls, *hey, we don't dance for free throw money*. So we all threw some dollar bills for fun and they shouted to Will to play another song and he started playing. We were eating and drinking and having a great time."

"We didn't actually notice that Ben wasn't in the group. He wasn't the only one. A few others were kind of the quiet types, and liked to just wander in the rainforest. But thinking back, Ben wasn't there during the dance. This was after we had eaten, and had drinks, and, well, I confess, some were smoking pot. This is off the record, right?"

"Mr. Radcliff, this is not 60 minutes. I'm a detective. So anything… but no I'm not actually that interested in your pot."

"It was right after the second song that we noticed Ben wasn't there, and someone said he had to take a piss and so he walked off. The girls did another number and then said, hey you guys, it's your turn now. And they had started throwing the bills that we had thrown earlier at us."

"So we got together and we decided since we couldn't sing, but some of us sang pretty well and, of course, Will could play anything on the uke. So we came up with an old song from the 90's and started to practice. The someone said: "Hey we need Ben on this song. He had that great falsetto you know.""

"And then we heard it. A shriek."

"It was then we realized that Ben had not come back from his piss. We, the guys said time out and we went to look for Ben. It was then that we found him about two hundred yards away lying on the ground. He was clutching his stomach. His eyes were wild, man. You could tell he was in distress. We could see he had vomited something. And, well, looked like he had some diarrhea. But then he was, like, very still, out cold. We tried to revive him. Couple of guys knew CPR. We dragged him back to the picnic area."

"You probably know the rest. We carried him out and down that steep cement road, it took us maybe an hour or so. Every now and then he would kind of revive and moan, and he seemed to be having like a hallucination, mumbling all weird stuff we couldn't understand. The girls were panicking. And so then we loaded him the car. It was Gary's car, and he was taken to Queen's hospital. But he was sooo still. Not moving at all. We all knew he was dead. Someone, I think it was Will, said I wonder if he had a weak heart? Like his father. Some of us knew that his dad had died at an early age when we were still in school. Well, Inspector that's all there is, at least for me. Any questions?"

Chang sat for seconds very thoughtfully. "Just one. Who did you keep in touch with on a regular basis? You know, Facebook, Twitter, emails, etc.?"

Reed looked uncomfortable. "Well, ah, not too many. Sometimes there would be an email blast. But you know, living in California, kind of disconnected."

Charlie made a few notes, then smiled and said, "Oh, and what about the first reunion. You mentioned someone died on that?"

"Yes. Her name was Sabrina Matsumoto. She slipped and fell off the trail. Died at the scene. Very upsetting to all of us."

"Was the trail muddy and slippery?" asked Chang innocently.

"Not really. Frankly, Sabrina seemed to be kind of out of it. Rumors were she was high on something, so that might have contributed. No one else had any trouble with their footing."

"Mahalo. No more questions for now. You will still be in town for a few more days I believe."

"Yes, I'll be here til Monday of next week. I do fly to Maui for two days tomorrow. But I'll be back, and will again stay at this hotel. I have it til I finally leave Hawaii for San Fran."

"Thank you Mr. Radcliff."

The waitress came. "Will this be on one check gentlemen or separately?"

"Put it on one check. It's a treat on me Inspector!"

"Very kind of you, Reed, but this is official business. We cannot be beholden to anyone and we never raise even an appearance of impropriety. I always pay my tab. But mahalo, and if I don't see you again, have a safe journey back."

AFTERNOON TEA TIME

June 5. 2:30

"Thank you Mrs. Conlin for taking the time to talk to me. Just call me Judy, Inspector Chang."

"I thought I would select a simple coffee and tea shop near where you were staying. I've ordered some green tea, but go ahead and have a meal. Been coming here to Cooke's for years now. It's a favorite hangout for officers. I remember coming here for maybe twenty plus years."

"What's the specialty here, Inspector?"

"I usually get what you see: the soufflé. Makes me think of Paris, although I admit we're in a humble diner in old Kakaako. Chef Tani trained at Le Cordon Bleu in Paris and made his way up to master chef at a Three Star Restaurant. But as so many local boys, he wanted to come back home. So he did."

"And I've never regretted it Charlie!" came a shout from the back. "You can't beat taking a short break and going body surfing down the street."

"That's Chef Taniguchi. His soufflé today has the local touch with the Portuguese sausages and lup chong."

Judy responded. "Okay you sold me, Inspector. I'll have that."

"Coming right up!"

"Well, while were waiting," Chang said, "let me thank you again for taking the time. I wanted to catch you because I know you will have to return to that mainland. When will you be leaving?

"Next week. I will make reservations in a day or two."

Chang gave her a reassuring smile and said: "Well, I'm sure I can wrap up the investigation before departure time. But please don't leave without letting us know. So I've gone through the initial police report. All of you gave the officers biographical information. I won't have to go over that again. So Judy, just tell me what happened that day. Start from the time you got picked up."

"So we went up the Round Top side to the top of the mountain. Stopped at Puu Ualakaa park and the lookout there. Then we drove up and over to the Hogsback – you know what I referring to? That narrow, one-lane stretch where you can look out towards Pearl Harbor, the airport, and even Tripler. Parked near the trail head, the one that goes off toward Nuuanu Reservoir, and we started that short but really steep hike up the cement maintenance road for the utilities. We got to the bamboo grove and walked for I'd say ten to fifteen minutes. We made it to the bamboo clearing."

"Well, we all sat down in the shaded area. We were just having fun, eating, fooling around with Hula. Sharing pictures of our families. It was then we realized that Ben was missing. Then we heard this horrible yell. The boys went to look for Ben. It was there that we found him lying on the ground. We tried to revive him. We dragged him down the road to the car. He was in and out of consciousness. Pasty look to his face. Bug eyed. It was awful. I'm glad I wasn't in the car that took him to the hospital. We were so upset. And we were all thinking that our class was somehow jinxed or something. Ten years earlier our friend fell to her death."

"I think that's about it. While we were at the hospital, we decided at least those of us from the mainland, that we would wait until we heard about funeral plans. Ben didn't have much family left. There was a chance it might be held in a week or so. We all said we would wait. That's how close we all were, Mr. Chang. Now of course, it may take a while. But we'll be back. I know I speak for Reed and others."

Chef Tani came out personally. "Anyone for pie?"

"No, Jonathan. On duty you know."

"Ha! Yeah Charlie---on duty. Haven't heard that one in a while."

"I'll pass too. I've got to watch the calories as I get older you know. We women can't take chances."

"Now you, I believe," the chef said as he handed out separate checks. "But it seems to me that you've got calories to spare," giving her a big smile.

"Oh let me get that!"

Chef answered, "No lady. Charlie is very good about that. He always pays. Not like some others. But then I don't mind. I've never had trouble in this neighborhood."

"Well thank you Inspector for that great recommendation for breakfast and for picking a place I can walk to from my folks' condo. Chef Taniguchi, I know I'll see you again and next time I'll bring the folks. They need to get out more often. Though I'll have to drive them. It's a little too far for dad."

* * *

A total of 12 interviews in two days. *Amazing how exhausting it can be just speaking with people.*

He went over in his mind the various conversations that he had had with each. He checked his notes to see if there were any inconsistencies or discrepancies, in times, events, who was riding with who. The next one after Conlin was Jarrett Tanji. *Lucky he was willing to come into town during his lunch break.* They met at Kinko's restaurant in Kaimuki. Chang had the special of kalua pig. Well it was lunchtime after all.

Jarrett confirmed the same basic tale. They started up to Round Top, stopping at the Manoa Valley look out. Stayed about a half hour, taking in the sights of the valley. There were also some memories that came from seeing the valley down to the University. Three-fourths of the folks had gone to the UH. They stopped at Puu Ualaakaa Park. They found parking at the top where they call the hogsback, and began their walk up the utility road. He was found about 200 yards away. He couldn't be revived and was carried down to cars and taken to hospital where he was officially pronounced dead.

Just like the other two stories. At least the lunch at Kinny's was great though Chang had asked for only one serving this time.

* * *

Yesterday. Let's see who was in it. Chang checked his notes. Oh yeah, Shirley Garcia. Kalihi girl. Met at Helen's in Kalihi Kai. Too early for their humungous saimin bowl and it was breakfast. Order of toast and two eggs over hard. Shirley had standard Portuguese sausage and char sui three egg omelet. She really knows how to hurt a guy who's just having toast. Began with the same old yada yada. Up the hill with the two stops to remember old times. Then to the top of the world through bamboo forest! Find the meadow and everyone is happy til Ben goes missing. Dies again. Same story.

Chang had to hit the country folks yesterday. So he started with Jarrett. Met at Hiro's in Waimalu. Though it wasn't lunch time with all that driving so a bowl of saimin was in order. Jarrett was ditto ditto ditto ditto. At least, Chang thought *I got a malasada after that light. Thank God for Lenny's. It wasn't a complete waste of time.*

Next, Gary Hoe, who was in Waianae, but was willing to meet with Chang halfway. So Chang suggested Leeward Drive Diner where he could have their house specialty oxtail soup. Gary had a roast pork plate but served Chang more Yada Yada Yada.

C H A P T E R   1 2

THE LAWYER AND THE FORESTER

June 6. Noon

Charlie sat on the flat marble wall at Honolulu's downtown urban, cement park. Surrounded by tall buildings filled with lawyers, Tamarind Park was an informal gathering place for casual professionals to eat their sandwiches and drink their Grande skinny latte coffees during lunchtime. He kept thinking about the other ten interviews.

He waited for Sarah Taira. Local girl, top of her class at Cleveland High, graduate of the Richards Law School. "Sorry I'm a little late," apologized Sarah, wearing the usual uniform of professional women, a light pantsuit with high heels.

"Going to Court today?"

"No, just a meeting with a high priced client. I'm glad you called. As an attorney, I thought I might have a different set of eyes and interpretation for what happened during the hike."

"Oh?" answered Charlie. *I hope I am not going to be treated to the wisdom of the ambitious corporate attorney,* he thought. Charlie knew that Sarah had been a candidate for the state legislature, and while not successful, she was believed to be thinking about running for prosecutor.

She quickly gave him the chronological facts of the case and her involvement. She got picked up by Maya at such and such a time. Next, off to Round Top, first the lookout then the park and on to the mountain. They hiked up, through the bamboo then to the picnic clearing. Talk story, dance hula, Ben went shi-shi. Boys were going to give concert when they went to look for Ben, cause he was taking a long leak. Found him, carried him down, then off to Queen's. She ticked off each factoid, as if rehearsed.

"Anything stand out, from your perspective as either a classmate or an attorney?" asked Charlie.

"What stands out is that nothing stands out. Thinking about that day, I don't remember anyone acting suspiciously, or differently than I'd expected. They all seemed genuinely shocked, and shaken, as far as I can see."

"Had you kept in close touch with them over the years?"

"Well, you have me there. I admit that after law school I lived in my own world of a young attorney. I had married, but I was so wrapped up in trying to make it big, my marriage kind of fell apart. We are still friends, but Rodney just could not live with someone who was, well, not really there, even when I was there."

"Were you aware of any of your classmates abusing prescription drugs or that Ben might have been distributing them?"

"I'd be lying if I said no. Ben had once approached me. I told him not to call me again. But I should have reported him. I didn't. You know, classmates, and all that."

"If you don't mind, do you, or have you ever had one of your classmates as a client?"

"If I do, or If I had, I probably should not talk about it."

"Ms. Taira, I hope you don't have such a low opinion of all police detectives. We both know that any criminal or civil case documents will have the representing attorney identified. So why don't you just tell me why we found your name connected to plea agreement several years ago for Mr. Ben Flores?"

"Ok. Yes. It was a favor. Ben had many troubles. Got caught peddling a small amount of pot to an undercover officer in Chinatown. So I negotiated a settlement and probation. No big deal."

"Thank you Ms. Taira. You have been very helpful."

* * *

Chang closed another hard day's investigation with a meeting with William 'Will' Kalaiopula. He met him on the grounds of Iolani Palace, the only real royal palace in America. It was a Friday, just after the Royal Hawaiian Band had concluded its weekly outdoor fortyfive-minute concert on the lawn near the Inauguration Gazebo. Will's story was pretty much the same as the others. Except for one thing.

"Were you aware of any classmates using any kinds of drugs?" he asked innocently?

"Why, should I?" he said a little too quickly. "I mean, did I ever see anyone using? No. Definitely not. Certainly not. Can't help you there."

"Not even pot?"

"Look, pot is kind of in a different category. Lot's of people…."

"Will. It doesn't help if you are trying to hide something, you know."

"Ok. Yeah. Friends. I admit it. Me too, once or twice. Not regularly."

"Do you think your former Cleveland classmates did much pot, or other drugs?"

"Well, I suppose some did. But I never actually saw anyone using."

"Ever spend any time in Chinatown?"

"What are you getting at? Do you think I go there and do drugs or something?"

"No, nothing like that. I ask everyone lots of questions. Just trying to get a big picture of you and your classmates. So, Chinatown?"

"I am not a fan of Chinatown. Too dirty and seedy. If I want a drink, I like Kaimuki."

"Ok, Will, you have been very helpful. I'll let you know if I have any more questions."

Will stood, said good bye, and quickly walked off towards the State Library building, just kitty-corner to Kawaiahao Church, the older Christian church cathedral in the Islands.

Chang watched him walking at an advanced pace. *Everything about this conversation seems a little off, he thought. Moto's instincts might be correct. If he's somehow less than the innocent he says he is, this might smoke him out… As far as the facts surrounding Flores' death, more yada yada. Chang thought, Will does have a mellow and deep voice though. No wonder he always bringing a uke with him. Hard to ignore the bandage on his hand. Said he cut it with a saw, cutting bamboo. Said he felt bad that Flores died in "his" rainforest.*

THE MANOA INVESTIGATOR
ARE HOSPITALS GETTING US HOOKED?

June 6, 2014

by Zoe Lee

A new national study suggests the growing epidemic of addictive opioids has been fueled, if not caused, by hospital pain killer procedures.

According to the Centers for Disease Control and Prevention, deaths linked to misuse and abuse of prescription opioids increased to nearly 19,000 in 2014, the highest figure on record.

How are hospitals involved? So-called pain management standards ask patients to assess their own levels of pain, a system that encourages heavier and heavier doses.

Dr. Brenden Krisak, chair of the Hawaii Health Providers Institute's Ad Hoc Committee on Addiction, says these practices have disastrous adverse consequences for families. "Too many patients leave the hospital with mild to serious addictions. After discharge, they pressure their physicians to continue the prescriptions."

"If a Doc says no, they go shop around until they find an MD who either doesn't know their history or doesn't care."

"It doesn't help when hospitals are judged by patient-satisfaction surveys. The hospitals want to get the best ratings. If it means being a little lenient about pain killers, so be it," he explained.

In Hawaii, the Citizens' Coalition for Responsible Drug Policy, a nonprofit advocacy group, recently wrote to the Director of Health. The letter called on DOH to include questions regarding prescription drugs on their annual survey, and to collect data on drug overdoses.

Tomorrow: Who profits from opioid addiction?

C H A P T E R   1 3

THE TURN OUT

July 6. 1 pm

"Well, I think the original idea was to make the Round Top – Tantalus loop a welcoming drive, with chances to stop and enjoy the fantastic panoramic views," he said as his arm pointed to the coast, Pearl Harbor, and the distinctive pink coral of Tripler Army Hospital. Alan Davids was the guy to talk to, so Zoe Lee made it a point to seek him out. He'd lived "on the mountain" for thirty years, knew almost all the older residents by name, and understood the rain forest.

"So, they call this narrow strip *the hogsback*, right?" asked Zoe, looking down on her narrow reporter's notepad.

"Yeah. You know there are a lot of wild pigs up here, so it is appropriate I guess. You don't actually see it with all the foliage these days, but if you look at the old early 1900s black and white pictures taken from a small plane you'd see a mountain almost devoid of any trees, and so the contours of the mountain were starkly seen."

"OK, so lots of people come up here, lots who don't live up here. And just driving around I see a lot of cars parked on the turnouts and lookouts, and they seem to be just sitting there. Is there something else going on?"

"Duh." He snickered. "Ever notice that some cars have a towel hanging over the driver's door? Or the combination of a towel and the hood of the engine up, as if they were actually working on the car?"

"Sooo...."

"So it is a drug operation. We call the police all the time, but Tantalus is just a small part of the police zone covering Manoa, Makiki, and Punchbowl. They can't be cruising up here all the time. Hard to catch anyone in the act."

"The towels are the signals?" Zoe was scribbling notes as she spoke.

"We can't prove it, but we all suspect it tells potential buyers when drugs are available, and probably which kinds of drugs, and once the contact is made, who to meet. Can't prove it, but it sure creates an uneasy sense of impending crime up here. Users need to support their habits, and one way to do this is to break into homes up here when people are out. Forget the dogs, a little tasty food, and the clever thieves can get in."

"So what do residents do, kind of isolated, yeah?"

"Off the record?"

"K"

"The residents collected funds to test video cameras posted on private property, to record everything during a several day loop. No official permission needed. Just private. They looked at different systems, picked one, and slowly they have been putting these up in hidden spots. If there is a break-in or incident, they look at the digital cloud to see if there are suspicious cars. Actually, these cameras can even catch action at night. So along with the neighborhood watch..."

"Do the police use it? Has it ever caught anyone?"

"We are not sure. It is not their policy to discuss specific crimes or whether they caught someone for it. You'd think the police would want as much communication as possible, but in the end, it is a oneway street. Anyway, they keep their organic and electronic eyes and ears open."

Zoe left her car parked near the hogsback and the cement road going up to the satellite dishes at the top of the mountain. She began to jog up the gentle winding road heading for the Puu Ohia trail head. There were always cyclists, walkers and joggers, so there was no danger of her looking out of place or suspicious. The black SUV was parked under a huge tree with a hanging lantern designed to attract and catch fire ants. The hood was up, and a red dirty towel hung over the driver's door. Inside, a driver slouched, with sunglasses and ear pods leading to his smart phone. She jogged by, pretending not to notice. Around the corner, she slipped into the brush along the road, hid herself, and began a vigil. It did not take long before a beat up rusty silverVW 'surfer car' drove up and parked next to the SUV. A thirty-something woman jumped out and went around to the passenger side, opened the door and got in. Zoe could not see much, but the encounter lasted no more than 30 seconds. The woman jumped out, and the silver car sped off. She tried to snap a picture as the car went by, but could not get the license plate. She did notice the tongue in cheek bumper sticker on the SUV: *Re-elect Gore in 2004.*

On her way back down the Round Top side of the mountain, she was stopped twice. First by a tourist, who flagged her down and wanted to know where the park was. Zoe explained that even though the Waikiki maps said all of Tantalus was a park, the only real park was one-third up the hill, just past the Manoa lookout.

The second time was to avoid nearly running over four skateboarders. They came screaming around a turn, nearly out of control. "Hey, illegal you know!" she shouted. They gave her the finger. *Damn kids. Moto says he almost ran over one in his Datsun, and a few years ago a skateboarder was actually killed as he went sliding under a car.*

Zoe Calls Moto

Ringgg!

"Hai. Moto here. Good observation. Zoe san, always digging, always watching," said Moto. "Moto think Zoe think the Tantalus drugs something important for Moto?"

"They are doing it right out in the open? Asked Moto. There has got to be something the police could do about it. It feeds the habits of so many, ruining lives, causing crime. Maybe this is something for Charlie to look at."

"Moto think Zoe be careful. Some drug people not play nice. Need more background on drug business, maybe check out Julie's bar in Chinatown. Tell Julie Charlie sent you."

"Not you?"

"She sweet on Charlie. But don't change the topic. You be careful."

"Yeah I know. I'll make sure they don't see or notice me. Will you mention this to Charlie when you have a chance? Oh, and guess what? Some of the residents have video cameras on the mountain. Maybe they can help. Thanks Moto."

MOTO-SAN GETS A HULA LESSON

June 6. 3 pm

"Moto hope Zoe like today's soba. I made o-shiru just chotto different."

"Oh, Moto-san, you never let me down. So creative. If I could write like you cook, I would be so happy with myself."

"You already best reporter in Hawaii. Maybe in this country – no blush, true. But tell me, you come lunch at different time today. When you come lunch, usually one hour later so maybe you run into Chang-san. But early for him." Moto was pleased that Zoe had started socializing again. It was two years since her boyfriend Kirk had died, and it took time for her to quietly grieve. He was pleased that she became a regular at his restaurant.

"Oh, my kumu hula has called for additional practices this week. We need to work on a couple of numbers. She's still trying to make up her mind what hula numbers the halau will dance….. Oh! I haven't told you and Charlie the great news: My halau has been selected to participate in the Merry Monarch Festival in Hilo next year. This is the first time for all of us. And though my kumu has gone as a dancer with her old halau, she's never taken her own school to the Festival. She is very young for a kumu, and it's only been two years since she started the halau."

"Moto hear about Merry Monarch. Wife used to watch when on television. She danced hula in Japan but not the old kind. Very different for her. Twelve years since she passed. I see hula, I think of my Kimi." He looked out the window, distracted by his memories.

Zoe let the moment linger, appreciating his rare show of emotion.

"Ah, she danced awana – modern, but not kahiko -traditional. Well. we will have to do both for the competition. And Moto-san, the amount of work that goes into preparation: new outfits, all those flowers that have to picked and sewn. And all the practice!"

"Moto think Hula good for Zoe-san. Keep mind busy. Settle broken heart."

Zoe became quiet. Moto respected her silence. He waited.

"You may be right. When I was really hurting over losing Kirk, a friend suggested I needed to keep busy. Needed to be both physical, and, well, spiritual. I had no idea how absorbing, how Hula is a whole world those not involved have no idea about. Or as King Kalakaua said, 'Hula is the language of the heart and therefore the heartbeat of the Hawaiian people.'"

"Are there a lot of these schools, these halau?"

"On the Big Island alone, there are over forty. Over twenty on Kauai. Over twenty on Maui. About 120 on Oahu. There is a web site that lists all these, and you should see how many are all around the world."

"Japan, too?

"Over forty listed! So you have this fascinating growth of Hawaiian music and dance. The ukulele schools in Japan, unreal. I can't claim to fully understand what the appeal is, but it is there. Maybe it is this genuine spiritual sense of Aloha. I don't know."

"Moto would like to hear more."

"Well, you may not know that the head teacher and leader of a hula school, a Kumu, is not just anybody. A Kumu always has their own Kumu, who teaches, nurtures, and matures them over time. If you are a really dedicated member of the Halau, you learn the chants, the steps, a good part of the language…then maybe, maybe, at some point *your* Kumu will grant you that honor. You can become a Kumu and start your own school with your own students, but all in the same dance tradition of your mentor. Kumus can trace their cultural and hula lineages just as one traces their family ancestry. Handed down from Kumu to Kumu."

"Tell me about the discipline. The sense of family, of ohana."

"Yes. That is so important. You don't just casually join a halau. You *commit* to it. You have one or two serious, intense practices every week. Each one is at least three hours in my halau. Our Kumu insists we formally enter the practice space with a special chant that asks permission to enter. We have our own small rituals. We circle. We hug each other. We come to understand we have been adopted into a new family. Frankly, I was kind of uncomfortable, at first. I was not ready for that kind of commitment of time and devotion. But over time, you change. I had no idea this entire world existed. Part of the special glue of Hawaii that newcomers cannot see."

Moto looked deeply into Zoe's eyes. He gradually allowed a modest smile. And a quiet approving nod."

"OK. Enough about my private life. I really have to finish this investigative series about drug addictions. Most new stories can be done quickly and still thoroughly, but when you're investigating something that people don't talk about and it involves really when you think about---ordinary people stepping over the line and having to deal with the criminal element, it gets tough. No one wants to talk and the police won't say anything except 'It's under investigation. You'll have to wait.' Now that's a lot of bull. In the meantime, more and more people are drawn in the web of addiction and from what seems innocent and medically necessary they get deeper and deeper into the drug scene. But enough of that. I am so thrilled about dancing on a big stage and several thousand will be watching us and we'll be on television. I hope you watch."

"Well, forgive me for just gobbling down your soba. But you're right about the sauce. Exquisite. Hope you have it again. I just gotta get to class."

"Been to Julie's yet?

"Not yet, but I'll get there."

Sayonara Zoe," Moto said as she charged out the doors. *Zoe-san always on the run.*

Moto went back into office with the two-way mirror. *Somewhere, where I put that card? Ah, yes, here. Bamboo artist on Rainforest Road. Help Moto decorate restaurant. Maybe pay friend Elmer visit. Lives on Tantalus. Maybe he has one security camera.*

C H A P T E R   1 5
AT THE HALAU

June 6. 6:30 pm

Ho'o mau kau kau! Instructor shouted and pounded her drum.

Ai! He inoa no awana, the three lines of women shouted back. They were in shorts and tees, but their faces were all business and everyone had a serious concentrated look.

They had memorized the Hawaiian. Zoe kept an English translation in her purse:

I express my love
For the famous wind of this land
Which I hold dear to me
The love-snatching wind
chorus:

My flower, my lei, mine to cherish
My lei that I adore above all others
You are a precious thing, a treasure
A lei to adorn my person
Beloved is that home
That home so delightful to visitors
Where I stayed and came to know so well
The love-snatching wind

"Okay ladies, we'll take short break and then we'll take up the second number."

Zoe had wandered over to where Maya was sitting after she had gotten her water bottle. "Boy, Maya that tastes so good after all of that practice. I lost track of how many times we went over that same number. Sure hope the King is happy," she said with a smile.

"King? What King?" Said Maya looking slightly dazed.

"Well, King David Kalakaua, of course. He single-handedly saved hula didn't he?"

"Oh yeah, of course."

Zoe moved closer to her. "Maya is everything okay. You don't seem like your old self. I know you're saddened over the death of your classmate, but you seemed out of it months before that tragic hike. Only it's more so now. Were you especially close to the victim, Ben Flores? And you told us about Sabrina, too."

"I admit. It is really hitting me. Not only Ben. Ten years ago, same group, Sabrina. Creepy, spooky. Like we were cursed or something. We were all close---the whole group. We hung out together a lot. We were together from middle school at Stevenson. We did everything together. The football games, the basketball games. Even soccer and baseball. Willie the great surfer also played baseball, wrestled and ran track. We went to all of his surf meets---out to Makaha, Banzai, Waimea. We were there when the swells hit 30 plus feet. Willie never backed down. In his senior year he qualified for the Triple Crown, the only high school student that made it that year and one of the few who ever qualified. We all went to the proms and dances, with our own dates of course."

Maya caught herself. "Silly of me, why would you be interested? I'm sure and I'm sure you had the same sort of memories?"

Zoe thought to herself: not quite - *some of us had to work hard; a single mom who held two jobs.* Yes that's true and I certainly understand especially since I know it was reunion time.

"Do you go back for yours?

"Well, not really. You know folks in Hawaii. They always want to have reunions and get-togethers including all of the many family ones in where else:

"Vegas!" The two said in unison.

Some of the girls pitched in upon hearing that: "Oooooo, Vegas, when you guys going? Can come with folks?" Maya said no, we were just reminiscing about school reunions.

Zoe said softly so no one else could hear, "That's why I haven't gone to reunions. Vegas never appealed to me."

Maya crinkled her nose and raised her eyebrows. "Wow, you must be the only one in Hawaii! Yeah we're very close. In fact, we're all getting together for dinner tonight. So many of the old hangouts have closed. We used to go to Wisteria Restaurant a lot. You know it was on King and Piikoi Streets. Used to be a big meeting place for politicians. But since there's a Zippy's next to that spot there, and it does have a nice dining room and private rooms. We decided to go there. I even gathered together my old yearbooks and candid's and reunions photos. I was pretty good with a camera. You know the old Kodaks. Do you have them with you now?"

"Sure we're meeting about an hour or so after practice, or when I think practice will be over."

Zoe perked up. "Can I see them? In fact, I'd like to set up another meeting with my friend Moto to go over them, if you don't mind."

"Of course," said Maya without enthusiasm."

"Okay girls, the kumu hula blared out. Get into your lines…. Remember one Awana and one kahiko. So everyone grab your ipus.

She gave the ipu a whack and the girls yelled out a chant in unison.

C H A P T E R   1 6

IN THE SHADOW OF THE CHOSUN DYNASTY

June 7. 10 am

It was becoming clear that Zoe's relationship with Maya might be a key to connecting the dots between the two reunions, and understanding who might be a suspect.

At Moto's suggestion, Moto, Zoe and Maya met under the trees at the University of Hawaii's Korean Studies Center. It was a special, serene oasis for Moto, who also often enjoyed the Japanese garden behind the East West Center.

"Moto Japanese, but appreciate old style artisans who came and built this replica of a Korean palace. Special carpenters. Special painters. We need to appreciate each other's art."

"So wasn't Korea kind of Confucian, a colony of China and then Japan?" asked Maya.

"Maya-san have same small knowledge as many others," Moto began. "Korea always independent. Different language, different ethnic group. Different culture, food, clothes, pride. Created own writing system by scholars – from scratch now. First to do metal printing. Last dynasty, over 500 years. Longest of any in Asia. If study Japanese history, can get impression Japan center of world. If study Chinese history, think there is only China. What is pure Chinese? Pure Japanese Only place three cultures meet – Korea. Understand Korea, understand Asia. Korea teach how to borrow, but not be eaten up. How to adapt, but not be taken over. Know how many times Korea invaded? Over 900, by one count!! Can imagine that? Who can survive that? Must be strong. Must be resilient. Must be proud. We meet here, under original tree planted when this building dedicated to remind us that we all biased. All see world through narrow glasses. Resist thought being colonized by the usual ways to see things. Maya-san see world through Cleveland High eyes. Need see through broad view, Moto think."

Maya took out her tablet with digital pictures of both Cleveland High School reunions, as well as the yearbooks.

"First, Cleveland High is proud to be named after a president who seemed to empathize with the Kingdom. But that is another story. Just know, a lot of Hawaii's leaders are graduates," explained Maya.

"Moto-san, please look at the yearbook picture folders Maya has brought us," persisted Zoe.

"Here we are seniors in high school, just before graduation," began Maya. "See. we're all here and I also have a few candids when the ceremony was over and everyone was giving leis and hugging." Everyone was so happy. Just pulled a few pages out of my scrapbook to bring with me. I have so many. And here's another graduation picture. We're in a group shot and everyone was trying to strike their own pose and some were horsing around as usual. And the usual candids with all that lei giving. Hey Zoe, how was yours? You must have gotten two armfuls of leis plus all the ones you had around your neck?"

Zoe smiled, but she remembered that she had only a few leis. All from friends and just a couple from the family relations who came. She went to a small school and having been raised by single parent who didn't come from a big family herself made it hard on graduation day. But It was fun, thanks to a few wonderful friends. "No one can forget their graduation day. An end and a beginning."

Zoe said, "I'm not sure why we should go through this, but I thought if anyone could gleam something from just a bunch of photographs it would be you Moto-san. You see things that we all miss."

Moto had taken the tablet and was looking at the photographs all along. There was no change in his expression. Then Zoe saw a slight, ever so slight puzzled look. She knew it was not the time to ask him and more importantly interrupt his thought patterns----whatever pattern of thinking he used. It certainly wasn't like anyone she knew."

Moto put down the tablet. "Zoe-san right. Something not right. Look at photo of 10th reunion."

Zoe brought up the photo and looked at it. "Well, it's their gang and everyone is horsing around, as Maya said."

"Zoe-san, now look at the picture of the 20th reunion taken, a few weeks ago. See anything different?"

"No I can't see anything wrong. But I admit I don't know all of the people. In fact, except for Maya have yet to see any in person, but Charlie did show me pictures including the one that they had taken on the hike. And I've seen some on social media."

Thinking of how Moto's mind worked, with much admiration, Zoe applied the lessons he had taught her. Zoe studied the pictures again. She began to ask Maya about girlfriend and boyfriend relationships. Slowly, indirectly, almost painfully, Maya began to reveal tidbits that might have meaning.

"Zoe, one thing I need to get straight. I know you are a reporter. A damn good one. I need to know when I'm talking to my friend, and when I'm talking to…well…"

"Fair enough, Maya. Let's set some rules. I'm your friend, and, as a friend, I want to know what is going on with you. But if you start talking about stuff that I'm working on, I'll stop you. I'll tell you if I want to change hats. Then it is up to you."

"Fair enough. What about Moto, here."

"Moto is just an advisor. Helps me see things differently. You can trust him. OK? Now, it seems that Sabrina was pretty popular with several of your male classmates, huh?"

"Are you kidding me? Half the class had a secret crush on her. Ben, for sure. I think he took her to the prom. Will also. Jake, even. To put it diplomatically, she was socially active, very active, if you get my drift."

"It must have been quite a blow to a lot of classmates when she died. I mean more than losing a classmate?"

"I think that's right. But you know, Sabrina was also resented. She was prettier than most of the girls, and knew how to flaunt it. She was not the most popular among us girls. Oh, we liked her, but once she started hanging with Ben, she was kind of a predator. Maybe I've said too much. Not nice to gossip about those who are no longer with us."

"I understand, Maya. And I promise, today I'm just a friend, not a reporter. Moto, we agree, right. Confidential?"

"Information and gossip confidential. Thoughts, take their own path to truth," he answered cryptically. One more question. Moto noticed this picture of several students, and one boy is holding a bamboo *kadomatsu*."

"Oh, that is Will. He learned to make them years ago. For a few of us, he, would make some small ones for New Years. This was before they became a real fad in the local stores."

Moto carefully studied the picture, focusing particularly on the level of craftsmanship of the "pine gate."

As Maya drove off in her 2008 Honda, Moto turned to Zoe. "Zoesan, Moto know Maya is friend. But Maya maybe in trouble. Maya may be in overhead. Maya may lead to others." Zoe was only partly paying attention. Something caught her eye on Maya's car. There is was again, that bumper sticker: *Re-Elect Gore, in 2004*. She forced herself to refocus on Moto.

"So you want me to kind of snoop around. Follow her? Didn't I just promise to keep things private?"

"Zoe promise to keep mouth shut. Zoe not promise to keep head in sand. Your friend may need help, so maybe you just looking out for her."

"Ok. Got it. If you think so."

Moto drove off in his fading yellow '79 Datsun hatchback. Zoe decided to stay and enjoy the calm of the shade, staring at the two story pavilion that added an additional authentic touch to the Study Center's Asian flavor.

Japanese art is so grounded in earth tones. Dark wood. Slate colored tiled rooves, except of course for the Hein Period, when everything was orange. But Korean aesthetics, so bright, multi-colored. Japan — formal, disciplined. Korea, exuberant, laid back, playful. I wonder why they are so different, she pondered.

As she was daydreaming, she noticed two men descending the stairs to the pavilion. Both were wearing dark glasses and baseball caps, so it was hard to see their faces. One was obviously of Asian heritage, perhaps Korean American? The other was more typically local, maybe part Hawaiian? Neither noticed her in the shadows. The Asian went to a Mercedes parked near-by. The other man, rather heavy set, left in a black SUV.

Her curiosity was up. She quietly went up the steps to the pavilion. It was a single, hexagonal room. No one was there. Its windows were latticed covered by white paper. The second level was a modest study room or library. A quick glance at the books told Zoe they were in a foreign language. She recognized the distinctive square shaped words of Korean, although she did not speak or read the language. A large round table with chairs suggested a frequent meeting place. There was a desk near the door, with a sign in book. She glanced at the book. Under the category: Member Reservations, she noticed the name: Chung-in "Jake" Kim.

C H A P T E R   1 7
MAI TAIS IN THE PARK

June 7. Near sunset

Fujimoto eased his fading yellow Datsun hatchback into the last row of parking stalls in the Magic Island parking lot wing of Ala Moana Park. He gazed towards the mountains, sadly noting that each visit was more depressing as yet another high rise blocked his view of the lush, picturesque Koolau Mountains. He could see the upper ridge, Makiki, and Tantalus, but the low levels, *gone foevah.*

He waited for his friend. Expecting to see Charlie Chang's vintage DeLorean, he was taken aback when Charlie arrived in a spanking new red Tesla electric luxury sedan. He got out and slammed his car door, silently demanding an explanation from his friend.

"I can see it in your eyes, Moto. Let me explain. No, don't turn away in disgust. My cream colored DeLorean was kind of faded, and there were those tell-tale tiny rust spots on the fenders. Needed to be repainted. Needed to be looking new again."

"Moto think you look too happy in new red Tesla. Having second thoughts? You are not going to tell stupid gullible friend this is just a loaner are you? Or, Charlie having male midlife crisis?"

"Not exactly. I have a doctor friend, brain surgeon at Queens Hospital. He collects cars. This was one he loaned me. Have to admit, pretty nice piece of automotive bling, eh?"

Silently they began their ritual Friday walk around the park. Recently, they took a different route. Heading past the new fast food concession, they walked towards the Ala Moana Boulevard side, making their way along the cement drainage canal.

"Look how pathetic our city is," observed Chang. Rusty stains in the canal, dirty, falling apart, filled with plastic food and drink containers. We are sloppy and lazy when it comes to our public places."

"No pride, Charlie-san. Lose track of important places. All commerce, no community," replied Moto. He stopped briefly to watch one of the large, strange, stork like birds with a long bill. It reminded him of an old cigar smoking bird promoting pickles. Also of interest were the ducks, with the mother leading the way for her seven tiny ducklings.

They walked under a strange looking tree that was filled with screeching and chirping birds. It was obviously a nesting place, but why so many birds decided to gather in this one tree at sunset was a mystery to both of them.

"Ok, Moto. Time to review what we know so far about this reunion case. We've got a thirty something guy who dies from poison. The same group had a tragic death ten years ago. Nobody seems to know anything as far as foul play. Their stories are all the same. What is going on? I feel that we are looking into a frosted window, can see outlines of people and movement, but it is not clear enough to determine just what."

"Charlie need approach from outside and work inside. Get inside heads of suspects. Passions. Habits. Patterns."

"OK, I assume you have something in mind."

"Because of hula group, Zoe-san is very tight with one wahine, Maya Kai. Maybe this our most promising camel nose under tent of Cleveland group. Also, keep feelings with this Will and maybe Matsumoto girl. Moto found a kadomatsu up on trail, and picture in class book shows same style. If Will still sad about girl, maybe he also still angry. Others, cannot yet understand. Just drifting thoughts waiting to land in one place, maybe."

They suspended their discussion as they entered the shade of the large banyan on the eastern side of Magic Island. Predictably, there sat the older haole couple, known to all as the Mai Tai's. Their actual names were Joe and Molly Davis.

"Lookie here, high fallutin cops in the park!" shouted Molly.

"Nice to see you too," answered Chang. Moto just nodded with thinly disguised disdain.

"Still trying to hurt us little guys? Stop those developments that could have made our retirement a happy one?" snarled Joe. The Mai Tais, who were sitting on picnic chairs sipping their mai tais from thermos bottles, were still resentful of a previous case where their two story walk up did not get sold to a wealthy developer.

"You know it was bad. You know he had to go to jail. So no grumble, or Inspector Chang here will arrest you for having illegal liquor in park," chided Moto.

"Not bad enough you guys kill our big retirement, you have to yank our chain about that phony award!"

Chang pulled his smart phone from his pocket and opened up the photo gallery. "I'd like to see if you remember this woman. I understand that maybe ten years ago she rented an apartment from you."

Joe and Molly leaned forward to look at the older photo.

"Wait, I think I do remember her," said Molly. "Member Joe, she died or something, and someone had to come and clean out her stuff."

Joe nodded. "Yeah, and that wasn't all. I think she was the one we were trying to get out because of drugs. Yeah, that's the one. Shelly or something?"

"Sabrina. Sabrina Matsumoto," answered Chang.

"Whatever," answered Molly, waving her thermos in the air dismissively.

"We just wanted to confirm that she was a tenant. It is important that whatever you can remember about her we would appreciate; you know…" said Chang.

"Now that you mention it, it kind of comes back to me," said Joe. Moto was watching him closely. *Joe always want to be important. Maybe Joe remember, maybe he just make it up,* thought Moto.

"Anything about her friends? What made you think there were drugs involved?" asked Chang.

"Loud parties. Motorcycles at night. Strangers coming and going at all hours. Can't prove anything, but we knew. We knew. We've been around. We can recognize these druggie kids. Not sayin we wished her harm, but when it happened, I gotta admit, good riddance," confessed Joe.

"Joseph Davis," said Molly shaking her finger. "Don't talk about the dead like that. It's bacchi, you know, bad luck."

"Here is another picture. Might have been one of her friends. Recognize him?"

They both shook their heads.

"It has been nice seeing you again," said Chang with obvious insincere politeness.

"Back attcha," said Joe. As Chang and Moto turned and walked away, Joe gave them the finger.

C H A P T E R   1 8
GRIEF FADES BUT DOESN'T DIE

June 8. 9 am

Charlie easily found the modest home in Makiki. It was built in the 30's, with the nice porch, and curved upper roof line. He parked outside the old lava stone wall, and walked past the cement oriental lantern to the traditional lanai leading to the front door.

An older Japanese American woman cautiously opened the main door and peered through the screen.

"Mrs. Matsumoto? Inspector Charlie Chang, HPD. I called a few days ago?"

"Yes, please come in."

Charlie was immediately impressed by the neatness of the vintage living room. There was a piano off to the side, and furniture that was clearly not modern. Glass covered shelves near the entrance to the kitchen held their most precious dishes and wine glasses. On the book shelves and sofa tables were an array of photographs, many of a young woman – who Charlie recognized as their daughter Sabrina.

"Let me call Herbert." She turned towards the kitchen, and shouted for her husband to come out.

When they had completed their introductions and settled on the stuffed chairs, Charlie thought it best to get right to the point.

"I am sorry to disturb you, but we are doing an investigation of a recent, ah, incident, involving some Cleveland High School grads, and we wonder if you might be helpful in filling in some history. I understand that your daughter Sabrina graduated with them in 1994?"

"Yeah. That's right," answered Herbert. His wife letting him do the talking. "What is this incident you are referring to?"

"This year, 2014 is their 20th reunion, as I'm sure you know. A group of graduates were on a picnic, and one of them, tragically, died at the scene. It wasn't like what happened to your daughter. He didn't fall or anything."

The Matsumoto's glanced at each other. Dorothy looked sadly at one of the pictures.

"Who died? Asked Herbert.

"A man named Ben Flores. Remember him?"

"Ben!!" they said in union. Obviously they did remember.

"Poor boy. Of course we remember him, don't we Herbert. He was one of Sabrina's friends. Maybe about a dozen, who always were doing things together. I'm sure he had come over to the house once or twice."

"I know this was a long time ago, and so sorry to bring up the past, but was your daughter socially active in high school? Did she date? Did she go to the prom?"

"In those days, Inspector, many girls went on group dates. They would go bowling near the old stadium in Moiliili. Or go out for saimin at Likelike Drive in. Have group parties on the beach at Magic Island, that sort of thing." She glanced at her husband.

"Listen, I appreciate the fond memories you may have of your daughter, but we really need to fully understand anything, anything, you might remember about that class. Those were the days when there was a major drug issue at the high school. Do you recall anything?"

"Yeah, we recall. Dorothy tends to sugar coat it. But those kids did more than bowl or eat noodles. They were kind of a wild bunch. Plenty times the girl came home late. Lots of em had cars. And there were more than group dates we suspect. In our days we'd drive up on Round Top and whatcha call it, watch the submarine races – you know, making out." Dorothy visibly blushed.

"Did Sabrina ever experiment with drugs? Marijuana? Other substances?

"Well, there was that time when we caught her and Ben on the back porch smoking something that we didn't recognize. It wasn't a regular cigarette," confessed Dorothy.

"Do you remember who she went to the senior prom with?" asked Charlie.

"Well, she was a shy girl," offered Dorothy, sheepishly.

"Bullshit, scuze the language Inspector. As a junior, she went to the junior prom with a nice Hawaiian boy, Will or Bill something. He really had a crush on her. Seemed respectful when they left. But when she came home, she was really upset."

Dorothy continued the story. "We were in bed but heard some shouting outside. Heard the back door slam. She went straight to her room. I got up and tried to talk to her, but she locked the door. Next day, she refused to talk about it, but just said she and the boy had an argument and it kind of ruined her night. So when it came to the senior prom, the same boy wanted to ask her out, but he had competition. This Ben boy wanted to take her too. She was pretty upset. So in the end, she didn't go."

"Such a shame to miss your senior prom," she whispered.

"Okay, so now we are after high school. Your daughter went to UH, right?"

"Well," continued the mother, "she started at Manoa, was going to be a nurse. A good profession. But then, for some reason, she dropped out. Worked at Zippy's a year or two, then enrolled in Kapiolani Community College. Took her a couple of years but she got her AA in accounting."

"Now Dorothy is leaving out some parts. Sabrina was still hanging out with her high school gang, and God knows who else, and after more than one argument, she moved out and took an apartment down in Kakaako. Seedy little place. We'd see her here maybe once a month.

Hard on the wife, after your only child, your only daughter, had lived here all her life. See her every day. Good grades. Piano lessons. Eat meals together, then poof. Gone. Hardly came home. In and out to pick up this or that. No time to have dinner. Hard."

"She would have been thirty-nine this August," said Dorothy quietly.

"Did you notice anything else about her behavior or friends?

"Unbelievable," said Herbert. "She got thinner. You could see bags under her eyes like she wasn't sleeping. Seemed kind of distant, what the kids would say – spaced out."

"Do you think she was doing drugs?" probed Chang.

"Oh yeah. And we confronted her about it. But she wouldn't talk about it. The more we demanded or scolded, the less she came over to the house. I don't know much about drugs Inspector, but I'd say the daughter that fell off that cliff was not the same girl we raised in this very house. We are a respectable, conservative, law abiding family. I served in the Korean War. I worked for the State Department of Transportation for forty years. Mom taught third grade for all her life in the public schools. Now she volunteers at Makiki Library and the Japanese Cultural Center. Respectable. I have no idea what we did wrong with that girl." Dorothy was dabbing her eyes with her handkerchief.

"Listen, I want you know, you have my word, that everything you tell me is confidential. Your private family life is your private life. But we have to do our jobs. We have to find out if there was anything about Sabrina's life, or lifestyle, or death, that is somehow linked to the death of Mr. Flores."

"So Inspector, I'm guessing that Flores did not just fall over with a heart attack or get run over crossing the street at Holiday Mart. I'm guessing you think somebody killed him."

"Herbert! Really!" said Dorothy.

"Well, I'm not surprised. This kid was in trouble from middle school. This kid, maybe you already know, was adopted, then the foster parents were divorced, then his foster father left the state and the foster Mom I heard died fairly young from cancer. That was after high school, right mom?"

"What Herbert says is true. Tell the truth, many of the high school parents were concerned about Ben, both for him, but also fearing his influence on our kids. He was wild, reckless, even rumored to get a girl pregnant from another school. We warned Sabbie not to have anything to do with him, but she said he wasn't as bad as people said. That he was gentle, and misunderstood. Yes, we did worry."

"Thank you for your time, and your openness. As I mentioned over the phone, we don't have anything new to tell you about your daughter's tragic death. But if something should come up, we'll let you know."

The Matsumotos escorted Chang out to the porch, and watched his fancy car drive away. Not a usually emotional man, Herbert hugged his wife, right out in the open on the porch.

THE MANOA INVESTIGATOR
LEGISLATURE CONCERNED ABOUT OPIOIDS

June 8

by Zoe Lee

In 2014, the Hawaii State Legislature passed a bill that stated addiction to and overdoses of opioid prescriptions "are at epidemic levels." This is the language of the Conference Committee Report on Senate Bill 2361.

"This is not a bill to prevent overdoses, but to treat them and limit the serious consequences," said Representative Dora Ann Cappuccino. "We found that there are specific drugs, called opioid antagaonists, that can save a person's life if administered in time. We wanted to ensure that pharmacists, emergency medical folks, and first responders would not be at risk for being sued if they administered these drugs to a person who OD's on opioid."

Cappucino acknowledged that while chrystal meth is still a huge problem in Hawaii, "the opioid epidemic on the mainland is coming to our state, no ifs, whats or buts."

Studies have found that providing opioid overdose training and kits can help people identify signs of an opioid-related overdose and prevent tragic deaths.

THE MANOA INVESTIGATOR has learned that several high school counsellors have expressed a concern to the Hawaii Department of Education that truancy levels are rising in part due to drug use among high school seniors, and that older students and college students are selling opioids to their younger peers.

"We cannot just sit idle and let this play out. We need to be more proactive," said School Superintendent Karen Miyagi. "We are working with the Department of Health and others to gain insight into how to approach this. We suspect that young people are getting some of these drugs from their parents. But even more worrisome, people in their twenties and thirties have access on their own. Hospitals have actually been dealing with it for over a decade. Unfortunately, it is starting to trickle down to younger and younger users," she said.

It remains to be seen whether SB 2361 is too much of a temporary band aid to make a difference.

C H A P T E R 1 9
RE-ELECT GORE IN 2004

June 8. 2 pm

"**I**nspector Chang your appointment is here."

It was the receptionist. Chang knew Maya had reported as promised. He had called her the evening before and made arrangements to see her. He offered to come to her workplace, but Maya said she was coming into Honolulu for a few appointments including one with her doctor. His office was just a block or two away.

Yes, Ms. Theresa. Honorable Chang here. Your voice is a half octave higher than usual. Inspector Chang likes to believe women get giddy when they get to address this miserable public servant. However as humble detective, Honorable Chang believe Ms. Theresa has, how you say--hot date tonight?" He heard a giggle and smiled.

"Oh Charlie, you always like to kid me. Ms. Maya Kai is here. She said she had set up an appointment with you. Shall I send her in?"

"Please do, and hold all my calls till she leaves. I am estimating a half hour should be enough."

Inspector Chang waited for a few minutes because of the required protocol and regulations. There was a knock on the door. The corporal on duty escorted her in, saying: "Hear she is, Inspector. Anything I can do or get you folks."

Both said no.

Chang began his routine. He first sought to make the person feel relaxed. "Thank you for taking the time to come, Ms. Kai. There's still much to do on this case and it has puzzled everyone in the department.

I must admit that. But I believe, with some more information, Charlie Chang will get to the bottom of this. I won't take more than a half hour of your time. I have just a few simple questions. Just to let you know, we are doing the same thing with others in your group. But anytime you have to take a break just let me know. I can also ask the staff to bring in any libations you might want. We always have pots of coffee and tea brewing. And I must tell you that the Kona blend here is quite good."

"I'm fine Inspector."

"Now my good friend Moto-san said that he had enjoyed going over your old high school and middle school albums and snapshots that your group had taken in school way back then."

"Well, Inspector. I know that Moto is not a policeman, but I've already told him everything. I'm not sure what I can add today. Inspector, when you called the next day, you did ask to share with you what I shared with Zoe and Moto-san. And here they are the annuals going back to Middle School and my prized scrapbook of photos of the school years and highlighted by shots of our group. Now, don't laugh at some of the crazy things we did, Inspector."

"I assure you, that every group of American and Hawaii kids have done the zaniest things anyone could every think of. And just so long as they're harmless fun, nothing to hurt anyone deliberately or involving heavy drinking and of course drug use…" *no reaction to reference to drugs*, he noted. "Well, I know I look the other way. I have three kids of my own and they did the same things I did and probably more. I just don't want to know.

Maya laughed at this. "Inspector you're just a regular guy, you know. I feel very comfortable. I was a little scared, at first. Thank you for assuring me that I am not a suspect in Ben's death."

"Oh, no Ms. Kai, If that were so, I would have to read you rights and ask if you wanted an attorney. You and the others are just witnesses. But what is a puzzle is: Witness to what? Let me take just a few minutes to just skim through the pictures."

Maya sat quietly as Charlie quickly ran through the photos. He did seem to stop at several of the Senior Class photos of the group. Ben for sure. But Maya couldn't see who else might have been scrutinized more carefully. The Inspector finished and put down the high school annuals. He moved to Maya's scrapbook.

He said, "I see you have very carefully mounted and labeled the photos in this separate album. You also give a time line for each photo. I can tell what year I'm in and for each picture the month and year. Why, some even have the time. You make the job easier. And you also describe the activity. Thank you. I don't have such a scrapbook. The pictures that I have are all in some box somewhere and I am sure that at some time and some place I might come across them. I hope."

Maya laughed. "We had such a great group of people, and we had a great time together going back to the seventh grade. We also kept up with each other, even after graduation. This is why we always made it a point to return for reunions, Inspector Chang."

"This picture of five of you, Ben, you, Jake, Will, and Sabrina, interests me. You are all holding up one of those satiric bumper stickers from that election year. Says: *Re-elect Gore in 2004*. Want to tell me about that?"

"Oh, yes. Well, we were pretty liberal, and most of us felt Bush stole the election from Gore in 2000. Just a lark. That's all," she said, with a tentative tone.

"You sure? Just a joke among the group?"

Something about this adopted bumper sticker does not feel so innocent, thought Charlie. Seems like a tag, a kind of subgroup symbol, like gangs have the colored handkerchiefs. Need to look into this later.

"Sure. You know, it was not my favorite. MY choice would have been the one we saw near the UH, the University of Hawaii. It read, *I Break for Hallucinations.*

"Yes, I see. OK, and here is the tenth reunion group picture. Hmmm, let me find your twentieth reunion picture. I want to compare them. I bet none of you have aged more than a few months or a few days in the 10 years. You all look so young, and, I must say, that I have met many of you, and that's certainly true.

"Hush up Inspector. You are making fun of us. It's been some 20 years ---hectic and sometimes painful," giving him a thoughtful look.

"And you know Inspector Chang, the last 10 have been rough for some of us." She was then very quiet.

Then, Maya said, "Oh Inspector. I, of course, have not mounted the 20th reunions pictures. So let me give you this envelope with those photos. It's the ones I took. Since some of the others, especially, you know, its the girls who still take most of the pictures, even with all those smartphones and Instagram postings and Facebook posts. Of course, now I'll make the collection available and send it to our gang when I get done. But for now, I've downloaded and these are the ones I brought to show Zoe and Moto.

Ah, yes, here's the 20th group shot. You're at the same part of Magic Island that you folks were at the 10th. And I was right! No one has aged."

"There you go again, Inspector." But this time Maya had a big smile on her face.

"Now, Ms. Kai, I'm looking at the 20th reunion shot and I compare it with the 10th. I count 14 of you in this year's picture and we of course, include, the late Mr. Flores. He is standing with his arm around Will. But I see in looking at the 10th reunion shot that there are 12 of you. Should there be 13? Someone failed to show up? This was taken before or after the hike? Where was Sabrina?"

Maya's face turned very somber. She was unable to say anything for a few seconds. "No, Inspector, everyone who could have come did come. But yes, you're right. Sabrina missed that picnic. She was unreliable. Then, of course, she died. So sad." Maya pulled out a small handkerchief, and at the same time Chang had handed her a small box of tissue.

He gave her a few moments to compose herself.

"Miss Kai, I have, what might be to you, a strange question. Were any of your group suffering from depression? Anything you would have noticed, maybe a sense of melancholy. Anything out of the ordinary?"

"Well, sort of, at least I thought so. Of course, Ben was always off in his own world. Probably on drugs, so sort of a loner, you know, and when we met up this last time, even more so. Seemed distant. Didn't laugh as much."

"I see. Anyone else?"

"Well, Sabrina kind of. But I think that was the influence of Ben. But that's not all. Now, don't tell anyone I said this, OK? Promise? Well I know for a fact, that Will had dropped out of school once or twice and had problems keeping work. Don't know why, and he did seem to be ok once he landed the job with the Department of Land and Natural Resources. But I remember someone, can't remember who, told me once, he suffered from depression. Had to be on medication and all. But Will is a sweet guy, wouldn't hurt anybody, and those of us who knew or suspected, well, we kind of kept an eye on him. We'd call him up and invite him out every now and then. And when Will was, ah, healthy, well he would do anything for a friend. A lot of Aloha in that man I say."

"Thank you Ms. Kai, this has been very helpful."

C H A P T E R   2 0
THE "LAUNDRY"

June 9. Noon

Of all the symbols of racism, colonialism, and corporate dominance, none stood out more than the Pacific Club. For most of its life, it was where the elites met to decide the fate of Hawaii. Nonwhites and women were not welcome. Yet as Hawaii changed, so did the club, more or less. It still took a lot of money and a lot of clout to become a member. But a typical lunchtime would see all races and genders enjoying the refined, old style, kamaaina atmosphere.

Senator Byron Watanabe was not a member, per se, but he had many friends who could invite him to lunch and dinner at the club. All the staff knew his car and his face. No one challenged him as he strolled up the stairs, past the lounge, zig zagged around the lawn, and took his seat in the dining area.

"Hey Mike, good to see you again."

His host, Michael Furutani rose and shook his hand. "Glad you could make it."

Watanabe looked around, and asked in a low voice, "Do you think it is wise to meet like this? I mean, I thought we had an understanding."

"Truth is, Senator, I would not have asked for the meeting if I thought it wasn't important. At least I was able to get this table off to the side, and not too many people for lunch today."

Watanabe interrupted Furutani. "Look, I still don't understand why you made it a point to get involved in the investigation so early, and to ask for of all people, Inspector Chang. We all know of his reputation. I just don't…"

"Look Byron. Cool head. No one knows more about Chang's reputation than I do. Yes, I've seen him at work. So, why not get him to quickly find the murderer. Get the Chief on his case to wrap it up ASAP. Then case closed. We're free from any chance being discovered by one of the other detectives, or Chang himself. It will just be some kind of murder, because some old high school grudge or some playing around by Flores with someone's wife or girlfriend. And that's that. Everything is put to bed, buried and forgotten."

"Okay, Okay, I see the logic and the typical Michael Furutani devious behavior. But I still get nervous. I mean it's Chang - best detective by far in Hawaii. Why can't we get some simple bureaucrat type detective? Alright! Alright! I've said enough."

"So, the, ah, chef is around?"

"I've asked her to join us for coffee and dessert. She is well aware how discrete this has to be."

"Look Mike, when this all began, back when Wendy was injured in the car accident, the one that you actually caused from what I can determine, I never thought it would lead to this, the complications. The number of people involved. If you two had not been driving around together half drunk, maybe things would have been different."

"Let's not drag the past into this. Accidents are accidents. No one would have known that Wendy would get hooked on drugs in the hospital. And who would have known that your nephew was a pharmacist, and …"

"Yeah and who would have known that I'd be blackmailed by my main contributor to pull strings to get those drugs to Wendy. This could ruin my career, if it gets out. You can forget about me running for governor and helping you get rich when we buy your land for the new transit line."

"Byron, Byron, Byron. We can handle this. We can keep it under wraps. I've already stuck my nose into the kid's death, and I'm sure I can count on the Police Chief to avoid publicity."

The waiter came. They ordered, and ate in silence. Each lost his own thoughts.

On cue, pushing the dessert cart, came the head chef of the Pacific Club, Wendy Gushiken.

"Aloha Chef. Won't you do us the honor by joining us for dessert?" asked Michael.

Wendy sat down, looked around to make sure they were out of earshot from other diners. "I just got a phone call from a reporter. She's poking around looking for dirt and drugs. Says it relates to a series she's been doing on opioids. How did she find me? What does she know? You guys are supposed to protect me. You said you would Michael? You know I have a family. Why was I in the car? And these last five years, I've kept my issues, my needs, a secret from everybody. And you Senator, what good are you, anyway?"

"Calm down Ms. Gushiken. I'm here as a personal friend of Michael. Together we are going to deal with this."

Furutani took his time adding cream to his coffee. "Look Wendy, there is no need for recriminations. When I found out Byron had a nephew who went to school with you and was a pharmacist, I asked for his help. Even if you wouldn't. I am financing Jake's daughter's Punahou tuition. Jake 'finds' extra pills at the pharmacy. The extras go to another one of your high school friends who distributes them, for a hefty profit I suspect, to a circle of users. Somehow, a package of pills finds its way to this wonderful Club, to be 'found' by you, Wendy, surprise, surprise, just in time to keep you high and happy. Don't put that pity me look on. Of course, no one would have wished this on you. I know, it was my fault, driving drunk, and who would have guessed you'd come out of the hospital with an addiction. But we, all of us, are trying to cope. Trying to help."

Did you bring the, the package," she asked.

"It is in the trunk of my car. When we leave…but let's be clear, if you are ever discovered, you keep Byron and my name out of it. It is just an anonymous source. Understand?"

"You sons of bitches are all alike. Flirt with and use people, then throw them away. If it weren't for your greed and pride and lust for power, you wouldn't be helping me with my habit. Ok, I agree to keep quiet, but you'd better keep my supply coming, understand?"

"Or what? Do I need to remind you what happened to this Flores friend of yours? Don't push it lady. You are over your head."

At the hint of a veiled threat, she blinked, and turned a bit white, Furutani thought. Wendy abruptly rose and returned to the kitchen. She waited ten minutes, then slipped out a side entrance to the parking lot and went directly to Michael's Mercedes. He opened the trunk, handed her the small package, and slammed it. Without looking at her, he got in the car and drove off. Wendy returned briskly to the kitchen and then to the lady's room, where she had a good cry, then downed several pills.

SECOND THOUGHTS

June 9. 3 pm

Julie's seedy bar in Chinatown was filling up by seven on a Saturday night. The usual clientele was there, and Julie's shrill voice and laughter could be heard over the Duke Ellington CD playing in the background.

In the back booth sat two frequent customers who, Julie felt, didn't really belong in her part of town. To fit in, they both wore LeBron James T-Shirts with 'Cleveland Rocks' on the back. Their outfits were completed with Cleveland Cavalier hats and dark glasses. *Who you kidding?* She thought.

"Look Jake, I don't think I can do this anymore. You are not much different from Ben, meaning you are a sonofabitch. He got Sabrina involved. He lured other members of our class into it. Your hands are dirty, man. I know we are good friends, and I have always appreciated how you stood by me when I was really down, depressed. It meant a lot to have a friend like you, and I mean it. But, you know, I just don't feel good about this at all."

Jake Kim looked deeply into his friend's eyes, searching for how fragile he was. "Will, I know, I know. I promise I'll find another distributor. I appreciate how you stepped in as soon as Ben quit on me. I know you still resented Ben. Believe me, it is just for a short time, promise."

"You don't think I will get caught or anything?"

"Almost impossible. Look, I get the pills. I package em. We meet, and I give you the names of the clients and how much for each packet. All you have to do is drive up the mountain, put out your red towel, and wait. The clients know what to look for. You've done this what, ten times already, right? No glitches. Nobody is watching or caring. It's your job to be up there, right? And besides, I do some of it myself in town. Anybody asks, just doing a friend a favor. You don't even know what is in the packages, right?"

"I don't know. You see those Manoa Investigator stories about opioids? The media, and soon the cops, will be on high alert. Someday they are going to find out, and we'll be up shit creek." *I don't know why I let myself get talked into this, he thought. I thought I was trying to help. Am I disloyal? A traitor? A dupe?*

"Not to worry. Remember, we have a back-up crew. If we suspect anything, the skateboarders make the pickups. I know we only did it once, but it is good to know we have a contingency plan, right? Like I said, I'm getting close to finding your replacement. I really don't know why Ben suddenly told me he was quitting. I mean, just left me hanging. So I had to turn to somebody. And I appreciate that you were willing. My clients will be looking for your type of car, a red towel, and the failsafe is the bumper sticker. No chance of any kind of a sting operation or anything like that. And I have no problem with getting you your antidepressants. I know how some people feel about mental health. Make you feel shame. I'm not like that. I know it just another illness like any other."

Jake went on, justifying his actions more to himself than to Will. "Ben had his own demons. He was big trouble since high school. I should never have let him talk me into being his supplier. But now, well, you know, I got a kid in Punahou. Expensive, that school. I won't have anything left to send her to college, when that time comes. So yes, I feel kind of dirty sometimes. But hey, I'm not the one getting people addicted in the first place. I'm just taking advantage of my position to make a tiny little on the side. Do you know how much those drug companies make in profits? You know they have more drug company lobbyists in Washington than there are members of Congress?"

As the two conspirators talked, Zoe Lee was biking through Chinatown, her favorite pastime on an early Saturday night, before it got too dark and dangerous. Tonight was different. She had a purpose.

As she rounded a corner, she noticed a black SUV with that bumper sticker: *Re-elect Gore in 2004*. The one she'd seen on Tantalus, and the same one Moto had also mentioned. She pulled over, and knew at once its owner was probably in Julie's. She took down the license plate.

She waited, and eventually two men in their late 30's emerged. She thought they could be from the reunion group, but she could not get a good look at their faces. After they left, she went inside and looked around for someone named Julie.

"Charlie sent me," she blurted out abruptly.

Julie looked at her up and down, making her own judgements. *Too young to be his girlfriend*, she thought. *Must be business.*

Without asking, Julie poured her a glass of white wine. "Here, we talk over there in the corner." Zoe was surprised that Julie had guessed what she drank, but there was more important stuff to talk about.

"Thanks, Julie, may I call you Julie?"

"Cut to the chase sweetie. What can I do for Charlie's friend?

"The two guys that just left. Do you know who they are, and do they meet here often?"

"Once a week they come in early enough to get that back booth. I see em passing little packages and whispering. One, the thin one, only drinks red wine, pays. Only he pays. Credit card says Jake Kim. That's all I know."

"Thanks Julie. I really appreciate it."

"Now you keep our good reputation out of your little on line news rag, you hear? Don't need no bad PR. This a high class place. Don't want to scare away the clientele, if you know what I mean."

Zoe thanked her again, but had to chuckle about the high class bit, having had the misfortune of using the ladies room. Hardly high class.

After Zoe left, Julie was on her cell phone. "Hey, you big sexy hunk, when you going to sweep ol Julie off her feet and take me out of this hell hole. You an me have an understanding, a copasetic vibe, my darling Charlie Chang. Speak sweet nothings to your future mistress." Their good hearted banter delighted Charlie.

"Ah Julie, good to hear my special lady's voice again. I suspect you have something to report?"

"Yeah, your young Punahou thing was just here. I hope you are not two timing your Julie with her, now. Don't get me mad at you my Charlie."

"Report please."

"K. K. Two young studs come here every week, like I told you. Zoe girlie is hot on their trail now. Do I think there is a connection with those other guys? Better believe it Chang. Julie can smell that flow of money and drugs comin and goin. One who pays, yeah, Kim. Sometimes well dressed. Sometimes tries to pretend he's like my Chinatown patrons with cargo shorts, a hat and a t-shirt. I suspect he is the ringleader. The other kid, Hawaiian or local, heavy set. Kind face, but looks scared all the time. I think he is just bein manipulated, you know, by the other guy. Kim drives expensive car, Lexus I think. Local guy drives back SUV. Yes, you owe me for sure. How about some of that special scotch. Wait, you got to deliver it in person you know. This wahine doesn't want to forget the face of her future husband. Ok. See you soon."

C H A P T E R 2 2

THAT'S WHAT FRIENDS ARE FOR

June 11. 11 am

Ever since the Commissioner showed an interest in Wendy Gushiken, Chang was suspicious. There must be some special relationship, he thought. Sure enough, his administrative assistant Theresa Thompson was a whiz with the department data bases, even if the computers were clunkers. These days, nobody had a traditional secretary. Most professionals had their own computers. The most important people in an office were the IT and the data geeks, in Charlie's opinion. Theresa taught Charlie to search the records. She showed him the interface in two traditional data bases with search engines: a traffic accident that involved both Wendy and the current Police Commissioner, Michael Furutani. This was before he became so prominent and powerful a figure in Hawaii's political and police communities. The electronic file was sparse. Theresa confided that appeared portions had been deleted. In fact, the IT department was able to establish that indeed, it had been hacked and altered. But not the two names. No doubt about it, Wendy and Michael were linked, at least in the past. But this did not, in Charlie's view, have anything to do with the current case, at least not yet. The interview had to be deftly, delicately handled, he knew.

"Thank you for taking the time to meet with me Ms. Gushiken." They were sitting in the open-air covered patio at the Pacific Club, a favorite informal business venue for member when lunch was not served.

"No problem. We are between meals so I have about twenty minutes until I need to get back to the kitchen. What can I do for you, Inspector?" *First the reporter and now this friggin cop. Bastard Furutani,* she thought, trying not to show emotions.

"As you may know, I'm looking into the tragic circumstance of Mr. Flores' painful death during your class reunion. We are trying to put together a complete picture of what people know, saw, or heard before and during that fateful hike."

"Well, it was horrible. I mean, to see someone in such agony, and then die practically right in front of our eyes. I'm not sure I'll ever get over that."

"And this was just about ten years to the day after the death of Sabrina Matsumoto during the tenth reunion, correct?"

"Yes. Yes. That makes it even more difficult. Makes you wonder if there is some kind of curse on our class, you know?"

"I understand many members of the class were close, kept in touch, correct?"

"Yeah, off and on. It's a small town. High school friendships sometimes last a lifetime."

"Help me to understand those relationships a bit. For example, let's take, say, Jake Kim. Does he keep in touch with a lot?" Chang watched carefully for any reaction. Wendy rolled her eyes pretending to find a memory.

"Jake, well he wasn't anyone I was close to. But yeah, I guess he's around. The guys tended to hang out with the guys, the girls with the girls."

"Well, I was wondering about other cliques. Ethnic or otherwise."

"Gee, I think the cliques had more to do with income, or status, or whether they played sports or not. You know, who was popular, social, well known, and their personalities more than, well, ethnics stuff. We are all local."

"By the way, I understand you know our Police Commissioner, Michael Furutani?"

"No, not really," she answered, shifting in her chair.

"Wendy, my records tell me you were actually in the same vehicle with him several years ago and were hospitalized as a result."

"I thought we were going to talk about Ben."

"Now, I am very curious as to why you would provide, shall we say, misinformation?" said Chang, having caught her in a lie.

"Look, you are nosing into my private life, and I don't appreciate it," she snapped.

"Precisely. That is what the police do. We nose around, until something does not smell quite right. Your answers, your attitude, your body language, Ms. Gushiken, does not meet the smell test. Perhaps you could tell me what I need to know."

"I really have nothing more to say. So Michael and I were… friends. So what? And you can't force me to say anything more. I know my rights. Now if you will excuse me, I have work to do." She rose abruptly and walked quickly away from Chang's table.

Well lah di dah. Seems we have struck a nerve her, Chang thought to himself. Maybe she is embarrassed that she was with him at all, or maybe it is something else. Let's see if this leads anywhere.

C H A P T E R   2 3
TAKO BOB

June 9-10-11

Zoe Lee's training as a journalist was all about learning how to follow the chronology, the money, the people…connecting the usual dots of human behavior and misbehavior. Watching. Analyzing. It was preparation for traditional, high quality, investigative journalism. *At last I am ready to play the role journalism was meant for in a democracy,* she had told herself.

Yet, as time went on, as she was appreciated and rewarded in her job at the *Manoa Investigator*, she was also sensing a lack of confidence from her editor.

"Zoe, you did a great job on that education article. Lots of links to studies. Excellent analysis. Good old-fashioned footwork. But at this point, your skill set is falling behind," said Nicki Lombardo, the senior editor.

"How can you say that" We are one of the best on-line news organizations in the country?"

"Yes, and I don't mean to be critical, but in this business, if you are not ahead of the curve, you are behind it. I'm talking about cyber journalism. People are not leaving fingerprints, as much as cyber-prints. On their emails, in their postings. What once was a bad guy hiding his loot and crime in and old warehouse, is now someone hiding behind obscure servers, encryptions, false identities, disposable cell phones."

"Are you talking about national security? Russian's hacking into the State Department? Snowden dumping scandals?"

"That is part of it. But I'm not saying we are going into the business of national security. I'm saying we need to pay a lot more attention to using the same environment for everyday journalism. We need to get a lot more high-tech."

"I see what you mean, Nicki. But where do we start?"

"I've been thinking about this for some time. You know, it's not that we don't know how to do internet investigations at all, it's just that we are not sophisticated enough. Remember last year when our competitor noticed that a legislator was an employee of an organization that wanted to build a private research lab, and low and behold, $10 million appeared in the budget? Two and two together, and along came a series of articles that led to a major ethics scandal. That could have been us who broke the story. Should have been us."

"You have something in mind, don't you?"

"Well, yes. I have an old friend. He actually worked for the FBI, and then went private. He's an IT security consultant. Knows his way around the cyberworld. He owes me a favor. He agreed to mentor you, to bring you up to speed on how to add this to your, and our, skill set." *I know that look on her face. Dutiful loyalty to the boss but skeptical as hell.*

"Sure, I'm game." *I hope this is not just another of Nicki's passionate fads. What do I have to lose? Might be worth the time.*

"He is very protective of his identity. He uses a pseudonym. Prefers to meet only on line. Here's his card."

"You've got to be kidding? *Tako* Bob?

"Let me explain the *Tako* part. *Tako* is the Japanese word for octopus. His dark sense of humor is to picture a bucket full of crabs, slowly moving around, kind of reaching up looking for a way out, but not a lot of action. He says this is his view of corporations and many government agencies. So, in his world, you are improving things if you shake them up. His metaphor is that you throw a lively octopus into the bucket and all hell breaks loose. Every action that creates a bit of chaos he calls a *Tako*."

"*Tako* Bob, huh. Sounds like an interesting anarchist."

"Not really. *Tako* Bob cares deeply about social justice, weeding out corruption. He believes that government is the highest calling, but for it to work best, you've got to shake things up every now and then. All big organizations get too lazy, ethnically, even if they are public, or started with some idealism. *Tako* Bob makes his money on security, but this is mainly to pay for his hobby,creating constructive *Takos*."

"OK. But there is no contact number here."

"*Tako* Bob will be in touch. Trust me."

* * *

"Zoe Lee. This is a message from *Tako* Bob. Please log into this web site and enter a password that will be sent under a separate email under the title: Box of Chocolates."

Zoe did as directed. After logging in, she was directed to a chat room.

"Hello Zoe Lee. This is *Tako* Bob. I am going to help you become a cyber-journalist. Before we get started, do you have any questions?"

"Yes, *Tako*, may I call you Tako?"

"I prefer in the future you refer to me as *Sydney*. And you need a new cover name as well. I am going to call you *Fred*. I will also send you a new email to use in our correspondence."

"Ok, Sydney. *Fred* is wondering about the significance of Box of Chocolates?"

"To operate in cyberspace you must be open to your own hidden assumptions, of what is literal, and what is not. You must think through more carefully what you are saying, thinking, hearing and seeing. When you search, you must search with precision. And you must be very prepared to be surprised with results you did not expect. So, Box of Chocolates. A guy is walking on the beach. He sees a bottle. Picks it up. Rubs off some of the seaweed, and poof, out comes a genie. The genie is full of gratitude for being liberated. You have three wishes. So the guy says, first, I want a billion dollars in a Swiss bank account. And poof, the genie hands him a certificate with the Swiss account numbers. Great, says the guy. My next wish is a new red Ferrari. Poof, a new car appears on the beach. And the genie says he has one final wish. So the guy thinks a minute and says, I want to be irresistible to women. And poof, he turns into a Box of Chocolates."

Zoe hated herself for bursting into a laugh, covering he mouth, even though it was just a chat conversation.

"You think it is funny, Fred? You laugh. But there is a lesson here."

"How do you know I think it is funny?"

"Because you covered your mouth. And you dabbed your watering eyes with that facial tissue from the box on your left."

"What?"

"Yes, I can watch you. I can access that little camera on your computer. If I wanted to, I could tell you who you emailed in the last 24 hours and what you said."

"How dare you?" Zoe quickly grabbed a loose shirt to cover up her bra, as she was home alone.

"Just lesson number one. Sorry if this disturbed you. But you need to understand how vulnerable everyone is. If you have ever paid by credit card on line, or put down your birthday on Facebook, or listed your address, or contact information, people like me can find it, and find you. But you don't have to be invading personal space to ethically investigate public records. Just so you know. Now, before you read me the riot act, let's get down to business. Nicki said you are doing a series of stories on opioid addiction. So, let's use this as an initial training exercise. I am going to give you a list of Google searches for you, and when you are done, log in again and we will discuss it."

Zoe looked down the list. Each search led her to a public database that she had never heard of, but which she could see might be related. Search for drug smuggling arrests. Search for heroin. Search for drug convictions. *Search for importation of phony pharmaceuticals. Search for drug cartels. Search for spikes in drug arrests. Search for FDA enforcement. Search for crime statistics in Hong Kong, Shanghai, Macao, Singapore, Okinawa, Pusan, Osaka…etc*

What became obvious was that Tako Bob – Sydney - was leading her through a maze of overlapping concentric circles. He was teaching her how to track the movement of drugs, and the laundering of money. He was using public data bases to create an investigative strategy. But it was not a linear, go from point A to point B strategy. It was building a drug ecosystem, a web, a jungle of interconnected human flora and fauna. It was another way of thinking about the world, and how to understand it.

In their next encounter,this time from a secured web page chat function, Sydney was more specific. "Tell me about this case you are helping with, the one involving the high school reunions."

In spite of being a little surprised by Sydney's knowledge, particularly because she had not mentioned the case,she was ready to cooperate and to trust his directions.

"Well, there were these two reunion,each ten years apart… and…"

"Don't waste my time. What are the initial, potential connections between people and organizations that are involved?"

"I am not that involved, but a police inspector and his friend are looking into it. As far as I can tell, officially, the players are the police, a head of the Police Commission, and about a dozen former classmates. I do remember a slightly odd interest by the Commissioner in one of the classmates. I strongly suspect there is a serious problem of abuse of prescription drugs going on. But these guys, now in their late 30s, are not that open about it."

"Your first assignment is to find out what is publicly available on all the actors. And while you are at it, find out how much is on-line about you. You might be surprised. As you were speaking I looked up the names of your main actors. Chang,Kido, Furutani. What pops out is Furutani Industries. Furutani, LLD. And related affiliates, such as HK Imports,Malaysian Sea Transports,and, oddly,Istanbul Textiles."

"So what do you think this means?"

"I don't know what it means. You are the journalist, remember? But the other actors seem pretty ordinary. Not that hard to access bank accounts IF you had a warrant. Credit card purchases are another story. I'd rather not talk about that for obvious reasons. But, if there were anyone in this cluster of actors who stands out and deserves some cyber scrutiny, at least initially, it might be Furutani. I'd start there. And remember what Deep Throat said."

"Deep who?"

"Oh this young generation. Do your historical homework. Read *All The Presidents' Men*."

WHERE THERE IS A WILL THERE IS A WAY

June 12. 8 am

It became obvious that the initial short interview with Kalaiopua needed a follow up. For this crucial second meeting Chang, chose the Ward Ave Big Country Café, known for its good breakfasts. As usual, he ordered the fish and eggs. Will Kalaiopua ordered the big breakfast with two meats.

"I appreciate you using your lunch hour to meet again. How is DLNR doing these days? I know you have a new director, but the funding is not so good?"

"You are well informed, Inspector. The Board of Land and Natural Resources and its department have oversight of millions of acres of public lands, yet we get only 1% of the budget. We are all stretched thin. And we all know we can't possibly attend to all the issues that come up."

"I understand you are in the Forestry Division? Spend a lot of time in the rainforest do you? Probably know all the plants and their official names?"

"Yes. Some would rather sit at a desk, but for me, getting out of the office and into nature, it's a perk. I wouldn't trade it for the world. So I assume you wanted to talk about Ben? But I want to apologize for the last time. I wasn't totally honest. I didn't want to cause trouble for my friends. I'm sorry. I should not have lied."

"Yes, of course. Now we are filling in the gaps, the small things. Did you know Ben well? Hang out together or anything?"

"It was more than Hi and Bye, but we were not like, weekly drinking buddies or anything. Probably would run into him once a month. Sometimes we were at the same bar, and chatted. Ben had his own circle of friends."

"Some say Ben was into the drug trade, maybe even a distributor. Ever heard anything like that?"

"Everybody knew," confided Will. "It was more than rumors."

"Ben was not the first to meet tragedy at a reunion, correct?"

"No. No, he wasn't. The first, who are you kidding Inspector, you already know about Sabrina ten years ago. That was the real tragedy. They say she fell, but my belief is that she was under the influence. And the person responsible for that was probably Ben. If no drugs, no fall. And the prettiest, sweetest, kindest soul among all of us would still be alive. I don't mind telling you that I blame Ben, who corrupted her."

"I sense you had deep feelings for her? Ever date? More?" probed Chang.

"Look at me Inspector. Not the Robert Redford of Hawaii. Just a regular, awkward, local brah. Not in her league. She hardly knew I existed. But yeah, I would have given anything for a date with Sabrina. No luck."

"I'll bet you know all the best lookout spots along the Manoa Cliffs trail," said Chang. "I'll bet you know even where the tragic accident happened. You by any chance know how to make a *kadomatsu*?"

Will blushed. "So you figured it out huh? Yeah, I'm the one. My own private memorial. Who cares?"

Chang was grateful he had mentioned Will's injured hand to Moto. Moto told him about the memorial on the mountain. It was a lucky guess that paid off. Then, typical Moto style, to make the connection, he sent me a Haiku poem:

Kadomatsu gate
Sun goes down, darkness rises
Pointing to Will's fate

"Well, Will, seeing how much you cared, and seeing how you might hold a grudge against Ben, the real question is: Are you the kind of man that would act on these feelings? Could you take a human life for revenge?"

"So that's what you think? I'm not perfect, Inspector. But I'm not a murderer."

"Did you ever suspect that Ben was not well, I mean other than the drugs?"

"I'm into forestry, not medicine."

"So Will, as someone who spends a lot of time in areas like Tantalus, ever run across people who are involved in drugs?"

"I guess it must go on, but we leave that stuff to you police guys. We worry more about invasive species, or people building extensions to their homes without a permit, or controlling the wild pigs. I don't carry a gun. I'm a biology protection person, Inspector."

"Will, trying to understand who hangs out with who, here on Oahu. You close to any classmates on a regular basis?"

"Not too much. Some are kind of rich, kind of uppity up, you know. Maybe don't want to be seen with the lower riff raff. Since I started working at DLNR, most of my drinking buddies work in the department."

"Will. What I am going to say may not make sense at first. But I want you to think about it. We truly want to get to the bottom of what happened to Sabrina, and what happened to Ben Flores. If I cannot clarify this, well, there will always be a cloud hanging over all of you. The whole class. No matter what you all do, no matter where you all work or live, people will talk. The only way to ensure this does not dog you all for years, is for us to clearly understand and explain it all. Please think about this." *Is this message getting through?* Chang wondered. "Oh, and one more thing. You know the residents up there have installed cameras that can record who comes and goes. Can even see the license plates."

Will looked at Chang for what seemed like a long time. He said nothing at first. He almost said something. Then caught himself. "Ok, Inspector. I understand."

"Actually, I'm not sure you do. We have been watching you. It is only a matter of time before you are… implicated. You can avoid all this if you help us."

"I will…think about… what you said."

"OK, got it. Well, you have been very helpful. I'd buy your lunch but it's against the rules so we go Dutch. If I have any other questions, I'll let you know."

As Chang returned to his car in the covered parking lot, he phoned Moto.

"What? Charlie. What find out?"

"Continues to deny, still a bit evasive. But does admit he had a thing for Sabrina, and resented Ben. But, stupid of him to deny he knows anything about the Tantalus drug business. Everybody in DLNR knows about it. They regularly report the cars to us, but unless we catch them in the act, can't do anything. A little too uninformed, if you ask me. But you may be right about Kalaiopua being on the verge of spilling the beans. He's not there yet, but I think we are getting closer."

"Moto also have some news. Zoe report that it was Will's car she saw with the red towel up on the hill. He was part of it. And she also say Jake Kim involved, but you know that from Julie, right?"

"Precisely. So we have Will, Jake, Wendy, Furutani, and maybe the Senator somehow involved. Maybe Maya, too. I think the picture is beginning to emerge."

"See Charlie later, compare more notes."

CHAPTER 25
SKYGATE SHEDS LIGHT

June 12. 4 pm

Zoe always loved Isamu Nogchi's public sculpture, Skygate. A metal, abstract 50-foot-high, undulating gray pipe opening above a steel structure with a small round concrete base that invited people to sit, and look up, through that opening. It sits on an expansive lawn between the art deco, quasi-Spanish City Hall, and the high rise Frank Fasi Municipal building that houses all the city departments. It seemed to be saying: *Don't look down, look up. Aspire. Think big ideas.* It was such a compelling focal point, that Skygate was the center of many a public celebration, concerts, book fairs, and multi-ethnic food samplings. During the holidays, it was surrounded by reindeer and elves all lit up for the kids.

Zoe made sure she got there well in advance, unwilling to risk her friend seeing no one and changing her mind. Then she saw Maya, who waived as she walked up.

"Hey Zoe. Great idea meeting here. I always liked this place too."

"You can thank the visionaries of the early 70's in the legislature, who earmarked one percent of all capital expenditures for public art."

"I expected you would know the history. I admire your interest in these things, Zoe. But to be honest, I don't really care much about history. You know, seems like one darn date or event or famous person after another. Doesn't seem relevant to me or my life. I'm into music, hula of course, food, the cost of living. Just seems kind of a waste of time, you know. Anyway, can always look it up on the Internet."

Zoe wanted to scream. She took three deep breaths before trying to respond to what she thought was so wrong on so many levels.

"Maya, I hate to say this, but in a democracy, ignorance is not an option. You live in the most beautiful place in the world, protected by the best system of government, enjoying many more freedoms than most. You are a citizen. You know what that means? No, let me finish. To be a good citizen you have an obligation to be informed. To care about other people. To try to make this a better place for you, your family, your friends, and maybe in the future your kids. When you live in your own little bubble, you let other guys manipulate everything. Don't give up your voice, your vote or your values to others."

"Okay, okay. Sorry I brought it up. Let's change the subject. What do you think of my new handbag? No, just joking. I'm ready to listen to why you asked to meet. No, I really am. Don't look at me like that, or like I'm an idiot. I know that look Zoe Lee."

"Maya, I wanted to meet where no one could hear us, because it is confidential. I wanted to know what is really going on. About the drugs, I mean. About the connection with your class."

"Zoe, nothing is going on. What are you talking about, girl? You accusing me of something, or what? I thought we were friends. And talk about harassment. You, your freaky friend Moto, and big shot Inspector Chang."

Zoe took out her smart phone. She opened it up the pictures, and handed it to Maya. "Don't say anything, just look."

Maya's face grew more and more distressed as she flipped through a series of pictures of cars, with clear shots of license plates and bumper stickers. Others in the series saw Maya leaning into the passenger side of some SUVs, and retrieving a small white package, or Maya with several classmates in a parking lot. And there was a grainy picture of Maya's car going up the road near a driveway.

"Maya, when did it start for you? Was it an injury, or some other reason you got involved?"

"Ok, Zoe girl. You found out. So I take some prescription drugs, now and then. I'm not really addicted. I can quit any time I want. But it helps me get through the day, and sometimes the nights. Makes me feel good about myself. But I'm not an addict. And I'm not like a criminal or anything, Zoe. Lots of people do some drugs now and then, you'd be surprised. I can quit any time. Don't tell me you've never smoked pot or inhaled."

"Maya, I came to you as a friend. But I'm also a journalist. You know I'm writing about this. What you are doing IS illegal. You could be dragged into a larger conspiracy. Now is the time to change. I am not the police, Maya, but I am a reporter. If you are willing to be a source, well, my sources are confidential."

"What do you want from me?"

"First, I'd like you to tell me your story. You will remain unnamed, untraceable. But your story, is, as you suggest, the story of many. I want to shine a light on what is going on in Hawaii and beyond. I want the public to be aware of the dangers. And I want people to wake up. And, really, I want you to stop."

"So you've just been using me for a story? Are you really my friend?"

"Don't be stupid. I'm your friend. You know that. And I care about you and others. What these drugs are doing to you, girl."

Suddenly, Maya reached out and they gave each other a hug.

"I'm sorry. I should not have said that. What else?"

"I need to know how the drug ring, if it is a drug ring, works. I want to know who is really behind it."

"Gee, Zoe, I don't know I want to go that far. Let's just start with my story, ok?"

"Ok. I'll take half a loaf, for now. So why don't you tell me your story about this. I'm going to take some notes, if you don't mind."

They sat in the late afternoon sun for two hours as the Skygate shadow stretched across the lawn towards the Diamond Head side of the lawn.

THE MANOA INVESTIGATOR
Profile of an Opioid Addict

June 13

by Zoe Lee

She is in her late 30s. We will call her Jane. She holds a steady job, pays the rent. She pays her taxes. She drives a car, shops at Ala Moana, eats at her favorite local restaurants. She is invisible. And she is dependent on powerful prescription drugs.

How did it happen? A friend, she thought was a friend, at a party, offered her, in a moment of weakness, pills to make her feel better. How he got the pills, she didn't ask. But it did not take long for her to be not only dependent on the pills, but on the suppliers and distributors.

"I can stop anytime," she says. And you'd think the cost of the habit would drive her to ending it. But it has been ten years since that friend made the fateful offer. She has not stopped.

She is not alone. Across Hawaii, the Department of Health reports that opioid abuse is at epidemic proportions. The most current data suggests there are over ten thousand are trapped in the jaws of the pills. As *The Manoa Investigator* reported earlier, average citizens are often drawn into dependency if they have an extended stay in a hospital. Statistics show that addiction is most prevalent among ages 19-40.

Jennifer Poindexter, Chief Executive Officer for the Consortium of Acute Care Facilities, said "We don't want to exaggerate the issue. But last year our Consortium, representing ten hospitals, established a dependency advisory group. We will be issuing a report and adopting a strategy."

Back to Jane. Three times she has applied for acceptance in a rehab program, but there is a waiting list. Funding was cut by the previous legislature. So for Jane, until a slot opens up, Jane will continue to be a user who wants to quit, but cannot.

C H A P T E R   2 6
KAPIOLANI KONNECTIONS

June 13

Kapiolani Park, located at the end of Waikiki and just below Diamond Head, had a long history of being the center of culture, the Hawaiian aristocracy, and common citizens. In the 19th century it hosted horse races and polo matches. A special deed prevented development. In the early 21st century, it had acquired a remodeled open air bandstand near the Zoo, where ethnic and musical festivals drew locals and tourists alike. Along its parameter, aspiring artists put out their paintings and crafts for sale on weekends. On any given day, there was a constant flow of walkers, joggers, and dog owners around its 1.8 mile boundaries. At the Waikiki end, across the street was the Zoo. On certain days, park users often could detect a distinct aroma from it.

Zoe Lee, Charlie Chang, and Yoshiro "Moto" Fujmoto sat on one of the green, wooden benches facing the empty bandstand. It was till early morning, and the long shadows of the many trees in the park created a pleasant and relaxing place to settle one's thoughts. Moto was remembering the last ukulele festival held at this site, where literally hundreds of young musicians played their instruments together.

"So, Zoe-san. You all excited. Want to meet Moto and Chang. Urgent. So we are here. Why?"

"Yes, Zoe, you said you had found something that might be of interest in our investigation of the Cleveland High reunion deaths?" said Chang as he pulled out a small notebook and his pen.

"Several things, really. First, as you know, I have become close to one of the reunion people through my hula halau, Maya. And she is getting pretty spooked, with all the attention you guys are giving her. So I'd like to ask you to back off for a while. Anyway. For the first time, she admitted to me that she was struggling with an addiction to prescription drugs. I was not able to tease out of her any connections to other members of the group for this, but when I showed her pictures of her actually paying for and receiving suspicious packets, her denials melted away."

Chang looked up through the trees in thought. "This is an important confirmation of what we have been thinking, that the key to understanding the death of Ben Flores, and maybe the death of Sabrina Matsumoto ten years earlier, might be this drug issue. Although, Flores dies of poison, not opioids."

"Moto think it all connected. But dots kind of fuzzy yet. Just exactly who, when, where and why not clean in Moto's mind," he said.

"Moto is correct…." He stopped to wait for a group of older women out powerwalking to pass by. "There are several things that don't add up. I think we have identified why Furutani was initially interested in Wendy Gushiken. Our computer databases linked them to a traffic accident in the past. Is that all? Is that connection a bit of a dead end?"

"That's what I want to tell you about," said Zoe. "Do you know that Furutani has significant business holdings and links overseas? Especially in Asia, but also, interestingly enough, in the Middle East as well? If you follow ownership of this one to that one, you can see that he is part of a chain that reaches into poppy production, and pharmaceutical research and development. His drug company, I found out by accident, does business with HealthLife Pharmaceuticals, which, among other things, makes prescription opioids sold in the U.S."

"Interesting. Provocative. But connected to our case?" asked Chang.

"There is more. We suspect that Jake Kim is involved, not as a user, but as a supplier. For a while, I thought it was a small operation, maybe stealing pills from the drug store, and selling them through some kind of network. Evidence points to Ben Flores, etc."

"Precisely. He has access. He has relationships. He has need, with a kid in Punahou. Suggestive, yes. But I must admit, when you think about it, just how many pills can someone like Kim steal without it being noticed? A little on the side, probably, but enough to supply a wider operation?"

"That's right, Charlie. But I found something more. Jake Kim recently purchased a new Mercedes. You won't believe it, but he paid cash!! And, here's another interesting factoid. Three months ago, Kim travelled to Hong Kong and Pusan, first class. And one of his cabin mates was, drum roll….Michael Furutani…in his private jet…"

"Moto wonder how Zoe know this."

"Let's just say I've been learning about data bases, private jets filing passenger lists, and corporate reports to stockholders. No, I don't like Wall Street all of a sudden. I have learned that you can create a search program to look for names that show up in different places. Three times Kim and Furutani's names show up in the same places. I also have some former teachers who are still at Punahou. Teenagers love to gossip. Jake Kim's daughter is no different. Daddy's going to Japan. Daddy's going to take me on his next trip to Hong Kong. And all those packages that arrive from overseas! Yada yada yada."

"So," began Chang, "you seem to be implying that this Jake Kim, a lowly pharmacist, is swimming in a very large, very expensive pond for his salary and status in life."

"I think that is indisputable."

"Moto hear Charlie wheels grinding away. What you thinking?"

"I'm thinking we should contact the FBI and see if we can access the bank transactions of our Mr. Kim. I will also see if what we have is enough to get permission to look more deeply into Furutani. Let's indulge in some wild speculation for a moment. Furutani is somehow involved in the legal, and maybe illegal, importation, maybe smuggling, of drugs, including opioids. He could be the major supplier. Maybe the petty theft of Kim is only the tip of the iceberg. Just speculation. Just fantasy, of course. Zoe, you are amazing. And I appreciate that this

information comes to us first, not to your on-line paper. I'm beginning
to see a faint path of bread crumbs leading through the rainforest to
answer the mystery of the reunion deaths."

C H A P T E R   2 7
THE FINAL REUNION

June 14. 11:30 am

The Cleveland Gang, as Moto referred to them, now down to 12, gathered at Toronaga's for an early lunch. They had made arrangements with Moto for this special gathering. He said that if they came earlier he could accommodate them by an early preparation for lunch and he took their orders and gathered the necessary ingredients that very morning.

"Ah very good, everyone here on time," Moto said. "Johnny-san will take you to events room. Not used very often but you will like more intimate space. More easy to talk to each other. Now I go check with chefs."

"And thank you, Moto-san," Reed Radcliff said. "For those of us leaving today it will be a perfect time to eat, talk story and the go straight to the airport from here." Everyone else joined in a unison of "Mahalo Moto-san!"

At that moment, the faint roar of a supped-up engine was heard, and Inspector Charlie Chang entered the room with his usual, understated flare. Moto often marveled at how some people when then entered a room commanded attention, even without saying a word.

I am glad that you all could attend. I am happy to inform you that all of you living on the mainland are free to return. Our investigation is over, or as we say, pau. I will be filing a final report soon.

"So tell us already," said several at once.

"You should know that Ben Flores died of a highly toxic poison. The poison was derived from the Angel's Trumpet flower. There are several varieties, and the most potent was used. Generally, this comes from the pink colored flower, not the white. The poison is tasteless, so you could take a long swig without initially knowing something was wrong. Obviously, someone who knows plants, someone who knows which ones are poison, was involved.

"Who, already!!!"

"Yes, precisely. Who indeed," said Chang cryptically. "But the one who laced Flores' tea was…Ben Flores himself, with unintentional help from one of you."

"What?" shouted Maya Kai and several others.

"Maybe we should let the person responsible tell the tale. Will?"

"Oh no, Chang, how can that be? …You're making a joke, right?"

"I'm leaving; let's all leave and see what the inspector will do," insisted Jake.

There was the sound of a chair being pushed back. Will Kalaiopua was standing. Everyone had stopped their chatter. The restaurant was silent. It seemed as if the kitchen staff had also stopped what they were doing and what had been frying, grilling, boiling, and simmering had stopped. All motion and sound were suspended.

Will spoke slowly. "Some of you are never going to forgive me for what I did. A few, I sincerely hope, will thank me in a few years." Jake Kim was visibly upset, but he said nothing.

"I know that most of us were approached one time or another by Ben to sample his opioid pills. What you may not know, is that Ben had recruited some of us to help him. Ben was ill, and could no longer keep up his end. And the person who made it all possible was….Jake, our successful pharmacist."

"He's lying Chang," shouted Kim. "Will, I don't know what you are saying. Maybe you are having another reaction to your antidepression meds or something."

Voices cried out: "No Will! You're wrong! We'll fight; all of us. We're all behind you Jake."

Will simply said: "No." He was speaking softly now. "It ends here. Inspector Chang, I hate to say this, but Jake had been supplying Ben with pills for some time. After Ben began to lose his energy, spending days at home in bed, I let Jake talk me into a so-called temporary role. He had recruited me to step in. I am not proud of this. Some of you, and you know who you are, met me up on Tantalus to get the pills. I'm not going to name names today, but I'm sure the Inspector will have a nice chat with you."

Now some sobbing was heard from Maya and Wendy. Everyone else had their heads down. No one could look at Will or the Inspector.

"Ben was once my friend. A very good friend. But that was a long time ago. He got hooked on pills and who knows what else. If it had just been his addiction, all of us would have tried to help him. In fact, some of us did. I know I tried. But he refused. And we all would have tolerated that habit. At least those of us who knew of it. It would have been left that way."

"Then Ben became a dealer. All of his business plans and talks of becoming rich was simply that: all talk. He couldn't keep on track to accomplish anything once he got hooked. So to make money, money for his pills, he began to deal. His grandparents, who had taken him in after his folks died in that car crash in high school, gave up on him and he was told to leave the family house. Ben was humiliated, but more importantly he was helpless. But we all know him, he always had a plan. And he had sources. You might be surprised at his sources. I'm not going to say anything, but you know who you are."

"Of course his plan was simple: just deal with the pills. But that meant getting others addicted to them. He began with the easiest way he knew: get your friends hooked on it. He asked me, but I told him to shove it. I even tried to get him to seek help. I'm sure others did. He resisted, and was so stubborn he accepted getting kicked out his home and his family. They all washed their hands clean with him."

"So he started to make money the only way he knew how. Ben began dealing. I'm sure everyone here, living in Hawaii, was asked. For all I know, he might have contacted the three of you on the mainland. I know he took some trips."

Reed said quietly, "I was one of them." He then was silent.

Will continued on. "Oh, he got his share of victims, all right. And one of them was Sabrina. I didn't know this at first. We hardly saw each other anymore, not like in the old days. If she had problems, she took them to someone else. The thing is, I am kind of responsible for his death. He was dying. He asked me to get him some kind of natural poison, and I found Angle's Trumpet. But the kind I gave him, was too strong. It should have gradually killed him, not all at once, or so horribly."

The room was quiet. Inspector Chang didn't speak. All of this drama was playing itself out. Then he stood and said, "Jake, I think it is time for you to come down to the station."

"Chang you are crazy. I'm not a criminal. I have a family. A kid in private school, and I make a good living. You have no proof."

"That is where you are wrong, Mr. Kim. We have sworn confessions of your co-conspirators. Some very prominent people. And Will will testify to how you recruited him."

"And for the rest of you, you should know that Ben Flores was dying of cancer and he knew it. Essentially, he took his own life, but not the way he intended."

Maya was the first to speak. "Inspector, I would like to make a kind of confession."

"Ms. Kai, this is not the time. For all of you, you are really all guilty of misplaced loyalty to classmates. I believe most, if not all of you, knew what was going on. But you kept silent. You thought there was some nobility in not going to the police. But look what you have caused. More than a few are addicts, and maybe recovering addicts for most of your lives. One classmate, Sabrina, died tragically because she was groggy from drugs. But by all accounts, her life was already a mess. Ben Flores was dying of physical cancer, but all of you, in a spiritual way, were also suffering from a social cancer. And you let it run without treatment. Only a few could be tagged with an actual crime. But all of you are guilty of a social sin. Nothing to be proud of."

Moto, who had been sitting quietly, said "Lunch is on Toronaga's. But leave big tip. Staff work extra hard." Will had already gone out the door. A police officer was escorting Jake Kim to his car.

I BREAK FOR HALLUCINATIONS

June 15. 9 am

It was an awkward arrest. Chang and several officers strolled politely into the corporate offices of Furutani Enterprises, where its CEO, Michael Furutani spend most of his time, when not chairing the Police Commission.

"Inspector Charles C. Chang to see Mr. Furutani," he said to the receptionist.

"Do you have an appointment?"

"No, but this is a matter of the utmost urgency. Please inform him immediately."

"Charlie," said Michael at his private office doorway. Come on in. Good to see you again. To what do I own this honor. Please have a seat, your friends as well."

"Michael, a seat will not be necessary. You are under arrest for conspiracy to distribute federally controlled substances."

"What the…you've got to be kidding Chang. What is this all about?"

"We know of your accident with Ms. Gushiken, the blackmail you used on Senator Wakayama to put pressure on his nephew to provide opioids to Wendy and others. We know of your payments for school tuition to ensure a cover-up. I must say, personally, I am very disappointed that a member of our Police Commission has so disgraced the department. Please escort Mr. Furutani to our vehicle."

"My attorneys will shred your pathetic non-case, Chang. All innuendo, speculation, hearsay. Leaps into your own mind, but without hard evidence. Get real, I'll be out on bail in a flash, and your career will be kaput!"

"There is some truth to that, Mr. Commissioner. Except for the business of large transfers of stocks to Mr. Jake Kim's Swiss account. Not to mention the warehouse on Sand Island owned by Tuna Imports. Tuna Imports is owned by non-other than Jake Kim's grandmother, who happens to be in a care home. Her durable power of attorney is, naturally Kim. On obtaining a search warrant, how surprised we were to find, hidden inside of dried fish meal from Pusan…millions of dollars of highly potent medications."

"I'm not responsible for Kim."

"I would not count on your attorneys to get you out of this, Mr. Commissioner. You took a small group of vulnerable addicts and turned it into a major opioid ring. Most of them did not even know how they were manipulated. As we speak, pursuant to a federal search warrant, three of your business and personal computers have been confiscated. I suspect we will find even more interesting aspects of your business dealings in drugs. And, as if you were not already going away for a long time, we'd better not discover that some of those pills that ended up in hospitals were not full of sawdust or talcum powder rather than genuine medications."

Furutani was not spared the humiliation of the perp walk with handcuffs. For some reason, someone had informed the media, so this event was shown on the evening TV news across the state.

* * *

"Chang arrested who?" Police Chief Arthur Kido shouted into the phone. "This better be a joke. Get Chang in here immediately!!"

After Kido ranted almost incoherently for five minutes, Chang, who was left standing in front of his desk, was allowed to speak.

"Chang are you serious? Are you hallucinating? This could be the end of your career!!!"

"It will all be in the report. There is no doubt, at a micro level Furutani was financing a girl's education as an indirect way to persuade the girl's father, a pharmacist, to provide dangerous drugs, opioids, to Furutani's former girlfriend. She is still addicted. He was clearly part of a conspiracy in what turns out to be a serious, ongoing drug distribution ring. The center of the operation was the victim of the high school reunion, Ben Flores. So we have the pharmacist, and several of the classmates involved. A major collateral damage to this, you could say, were the classmates who remain addicted to opioids. At first we thought Mr. Kalaiopua had murdered Flores out of a warped sense of delayed revenge for getting his classmate Sabrina Matsumoto high, and indirectly causing her to fall to her death, some ten years ago."

"You mean there were two murders?"

"Two deaths. Actually, there were no murders. At least not the way we think of murder."

"Now you are not making sense Chang."

"This guy Kalaiopua did resent the role Flores played in the girl's death. No doubt he had thoughts of revenge and even violence. He went to Flores and confronted him. But then what happened was a twist of unpredictable fate. Turns out Flores was seriously ill, was dying of liver cancer actually, and he knew it. He was in pain, and even the opioids he had access to would not help. He could not wait for the cancer. The pain was becoming unbearable. He was going to end his life. Flores was a scoundrel for sure, but he knew that suicide was not covered by his insurance policy. Yes, he did have life insurance, and the beneficiary was his aging grandmother. He needed a way out that looked like something else. He persuaded Will Kalaiopua to help, sort of. He asked Will to find some natural poison, and make it look like he had like a heart attack or something. Will, agreed, but it backfired. The level of poison was much stronger than he thought. Flores' planned demise was not a longer drawn out fever, illness and death, nor did it look anything like a typical heart attack…presumably occurring well after the hike, but immediate, painful, and dramatic."

"Kalaiopua is your source on this story?"

"He was a source on a part of this story. Will was persuaded to work with us undercover. It took some time, but he finally recognized that by turning state's evidence on his fellow graduates, he would be doing them a favor. If we didn't break up the ring, more lives would be ruined. At first, we didn't really have a plan. What we didn't know fully was who was the supplier for Ben Flores. Our big break was when Will was approached by Kim to fill in for Ben. This was even before the reunion."

"So Kalaiopua was not yet fully recruited until Kim contacted him?"

"That's right. We had circumstantial evidence that he was part of the distribution ring, but not hard proof. We wanted to persuade him that it was only a matter of time before he was caught in the act. We had worked on him. So he agreed to help us conduct a number of stings up on Tantalus. Kalaiopua was easily accepted by the clients."

"But guilty of a crime, right? Indictable?"

"No. We were not sure we could crack the case against him or the others unless we caught them in the act, and that is hard. Anyway, his cooperation bought him a year of probation."

"Was he actually on the payroll?" asked Kido.

"Not in cash, but he suffers from depression. So we paid for his meds for a few months, and helped to enroll him in a mental health program. But this was not the essential reason he agreed. It was his long lost crush on Sabrina Matsumoto, who died ten years ago on the hike, and his desire not to see it happen to others."

"I don't fully understand how you identified the members of the ring?"

"We had help. Friends who know the community. Discovered one way of identifying each other was a silly bumper sticker. Most of the graduates no longer kept this memento of 2004, but not the essential players."

"What do you mean, help, Chang? I hope you didn't involve people outside the department again, this Moto character or…"

"Protocols were followed. But as you know, good police work always relies on good community relations. Confidential sources. More than that. Our IT people have been working with the FBI. We are able to cross-reference names in thousands of data bases. The keys as to who to look at and where came, I must admit, not from us, but from a reporter. In this day and age, it is usually not one agency or organization that solves a case. We all need each other."

Arthur Kido did not approve of Chang's unauthorized methods, but it was pointless to protest. Chang would always do it his way.

"So you are telling me that nobody was murdered, that one was an accident, and the other a suicide that got out of hand with an overdose of some natural poison?"

"Precisely. This is one case where all of us were wrong at first. We jumped to conclusions. So the only real crimes were the key players in the drug ring. Flores, Kim, Gushiken, Furutani, and, although I'm not sure it was technically a crime, the actions of the senator, who will pay at the ballot box."

"What about the other woman, Maya something?"

"Just an innocent who got dependent. She is just enrolled in a rehab program that provides another drug to wean her off of the opioids."

"Unbelievable! That report had better be long on details, Chang. But if what you say is true, then you deserve credit for being humble enough to change your strategy after jumping to conclusions. I'm glad this episode is over. You wouldn't believe how much flak I've received."

"Sorry to tell you this, but there is more, much more. This little small time pill ring was only the tip of the iceberg. It connects to poppy fields in Afghanistan, to off shore pharmaceutical manufacturing in Hong Kong, and to the unregistered and illegal import and distribution of larger amounts in Hawaii. And at the center of it was Furutani. I'm afraid, Chief, in no time at all you will wish it were only about some high school classmates."

THE MANOA INVESTIGATOR
POWER AND DRUGS:
Tragedy Hits High School Alums...Again

June 13

by Zoe Lee

The Manoa Investigator has learned that the epidemic of opioid addiction has struck the Cleveland High School Class of 1994. Drugs and their affects hit the class hard, with one accidental death at the school's tenth year reunion in 2004, and one more during the recent 20th reunion. It is a story of illicit affairs, an accident victim becoming addicted during a hospital stay, and how men of power and influence thought they were above the law.

The drug culture of the 80's infected a Cleveland graduate, Ben Flores, who built a small but lucrative business distributing them to his friends and their friends. (See our report of June3) Other classmates were his first targets. Lives were compromised and corrupted. Flores was implicated in the death of Sabrina Matsumoto in 2004, who fell to her death on a hike in the Tantalus rain forest. She was found to have high levels of opioids in her system.

Fast forward to 2014, and this time, Ben Flores was the unlucky one to lose his life. We broke the story that Flores had intended to commit suicide but wanted to disguise it by ingesting extracts of a toxic flower, the beautiful and abundant Angel's Trumpet. The idea was to induce death by heart attack. A classmate assisted by identifying the plant and supplying Flores with it. But it was so strong that Flores died a painful death.

These tragedies are further complicated by the involvement of corporate CEO Michael Furutani, who was Chair of the Police Commission. Furutani, also a graduate of Cleveland High, was having a secret affair with yet another Cleveland grad, when an accident landed her in the hospital. MI sees no reason to expose her name at this time. However, she emerged addicted to opioids, and turned to Furutani to find a source to feed her addition. Furutani was a major contributor to Senator Byron Wakayama (D – Tantalus District).

Furutani leaned on the senator to persuade his nephew, a pharmacist, to steal and supply drugs. Another life ruined when the nephew, a Jake Kim, went into business with his distant cousin, Park. Kim stole the pills, and Park distributed them. Many members of the '94 Class were approached. Some accepted the invitation. Kim took a plea agreement and is now serving a five-year prison sentence.

The bigger story was that Furutani was indicted by a Federal Grand Jury for illegal import and distribution of controlled substances. The Furutani cartel implicates agricultural holdings in the Middle East, and pharmaceutical manufacturing in Hong Kong.

Inspector Charles C. Chang of the Honolulu Police Department was quoted as saying, "Drugs are a social cancer that leaves no one untouched."by the previous legislature. So for Jane, until a slot opens up, Jane will continue to be a user who wants to quit, but cannot.

C H A P T E R   2 9
Post- Postscript…Kadomatsu for Kirk

January 2015

Hey Kirk. Still missing you. I brought you this small but nice Kadomatsu. Not many graves can boast of one of these. It was made by Will. You should see the two large ones he made for Moto's restaurant. Speaking of which. Both Moto and Chang flew over to Hilo to see our Halau perform in the Merrie Monarch Hula Festival. If you were looking down on us, I was the skinny one in the second row. Hardly look Hawaiian, but our Kumu always says it's not your face but your heart that makes you Hawaiian. Moto knows the chef from the new Hilo restaurant just down from the Kress Building. The one we had lunch at? So he made okonomiyaki for all our Halau members, Osaka style…it was your favorite…

Soooo, I wanted to share my big news. Moved out of my apartment and up to Tantalus. An older couple is renting me the downstairs of their house. Amazing living up there. All the water is on catchment. My landlady Michiko says her husband Jimmy calls themselves boomer pioneers. Of course it is beautiful, and you wake up every day to the songs of all kinds of birds. Every day it is a gentle journey driving down the hill, slowly entering busy Honolulu. And every night, you gently transition back up…careful not to run over the mongoose or the wild chickens…I so wish you could be living with me up here.…But I AM getting on with my life. I still need to come and talk to you like this…but your Zoe is going to be OK. I am moving on…Peace to you my Kirk.